Her sin, Jason could tell just from seeing that evil glow on her face, was pride. Blinded by pride, she could never have graded his essay as it deserved.

Which proved that his very first instinct had been the right one—he had to get face to face with her. Alone and in private. He had to make her listen. . . .

Ms. Milledge had judged him, and judged falsely. Hate the sin, love the sinner. He prayed for the strength to comply.

Also by Margaret Logan
Published by Fawcett Books:

DEATHAMPTON SUMMER
A KILLING IN VENTURE CAPITAL

C.A.T.
Caper

Margaret Logan

FAWCETT CREST • NEW YORK

A Fawcett Crest Book
Published by Ballantine Books
Copyright © 1990 by Margaret Logan

Library of Congress Catalog Card Number: 89-49607

ISBN 0-449-21957-7

This edition published by arrangement with Walker and Company.

Manufactured in the United States of America

First Ballantine Books Edition: February 1992

For Vivian and Tracy Logan

Chapter 1

*Human beings are born free, and everywhere
they are in chains.*

Jason Armbruster, like the other high school seniors in
the room, had never seen the short sentence before. Part
of the C.A.T., the College Aptitude Test, it was supposed
to elicit from each of them an essay that would demon-
strate their writing skills.

They were allowed thirty minutes. Three had passed
already, but Jason couldn't take the sentence in. Pieces of
words kept separating and swimming into each other.
MANBE, he read, REBO. INCH.

Be concrete, he reminded himself. Write an introductory sentence, give two or three concrete examples, and
summarize.

The test for Math Achievement that had begun this Saturday morning for Jason had been easy, a joke. But top
colleges want more than one-dimensional smarts, and
Computer Club was the sum total of his extracurricular
activity. An excellent performance on the C.A.T. essay
that now confronted him, Jason believed, was his only
hope against a heavy nerd factor.

He tried again to read the topic, a nail-bitten finger trac-
ing it out one word at a time. His mouth was sour. A
cottony roar filled his ears.

The minute hand of the clock jumped, loud as gunfire. Five minutes gone. Twenty-five left. Around him, the other kids scribbled energetically. The hot room smelled of chalk, young sweat, and the scratch 'n' sniff class of perfumery.

The topic swam and danced. He abandoned it and scanned down to the directions. These, G—d be thanked, were what Miss Touhey had promised. *By using examples from literature, the arts, history, daily life or current events, show that you agree or disagree with this statement.*

"When in doubt, use daily life," Miss Touhey had advised them at the end of class Friday. "Be natural and honest—your true seventeen-year-old self. Remember that real people, English teachers just like me, will read and score these essays. Write so they can enjoy their work when they come to your paper."

Jennifer Kress had raised her hand. "Is there anything we can do tonight to sort of get ourselves in a creative mood?"

The jocks in the back snickered. Miss Touhey ignored them and swept her large-eyed gaze across the goodies who sat up front. "What I'd do," she answered, "I'd re-read Orwell's 'Politics and the English Language.' "

Remembering, Jason almost cried aloud. George Orwell! A G—dless Communist inspiring his classmates' scribbling fists while he sat doomed!

The pistol shot of the clock again. Jason put his pencil down and laced his hands tightly. *The Lord is my shepherd,* he began.

His prayer finished, he opened his eyes. There it lay, clear and comprehensible. He read, and his heart leaped up. More than any practice topic, drawn from past C.A.T.s or invented by Miss Touhey, this one was clearly and undeniably *his*. For *him*, praise Jesus! A sign—at last!—that his terrible crimes belonged to the past, that the forgiveness promised in Scripture was truly his.

His soul large and powerful within him, he picked up his pencil and let the shining truth burst free.

The kids banged through the double doors of the old brick building into a gray day that felt more like snow than rain. Few had dressed for the cold, wearing, instead, denim jackets and sweatshirts printed with college insignia or identifications like "Brookline Wrestling." You could imagine their mothers, earlier, swallowing advice about wool or down, telling themselves the kids had pressure enough without being hassled about clothes.

Most were white, with a sprinkling of black and Asian faces. Except for one gregarious Chinese boy, there was little racial mixing. Earphones were common, cigarettes, in this enlightened suburb, not.

Four boys waited together near the bottom of the wide steps. The most handsome, tall and aloof, wore a sweatshirt with a crimson shield saying "Veritas." His older brother was at Harvard; everyone expected Harvard to accept him too.

A girl with animated features and messy dark curls waited on the other side of the stairs. Whenever someone she knew came out, she pounced with the same question. "Did you do *Gatsby*?" Several had used this example of a man in chains, each admission filling the air with fresh shrieks.

A couple of dozen kids had driven to the test, parking their cars on the circular driveway that fronted the school building. The newest and most expensive of these cars had been borrowed from parents. That any parent in a suburban American town would give up his or her car for most of Saturday said a great deal about the stressful prestige of the C.A.T. ritual.

Engines throbbed into life, tape decks set to the max.

"I don't know what I said," a boy told the Gatsby girl. "I totally spazzed out."

A tiny girl with a hennaed crewcut whooped at the sight of her crewcut boyfriend. Both were togged in black from head to toe. A quick, businesslike kiss and they were off, he carrying her piggyback.

The aloof boy in the Harvard sweatshirt snapped to. Tripping down the stairs was the prettiest girl in Brookline High, smoky gray wideset eyes, long blond hair.

She knew she was supposed to smile, to say something that would show she was glad to see him.

"What?" he asked. "What's wrong?"

She tossed her hair, her eyes vague. "Nothing. I'm just psyched it's over."

He nodded. Without another word, the two of them set forth in the direction of the Burger King, followed closely by their retinue.

Jason Armbruster was the last kid through the doors.

The Gatsby girl knew Jason from homeroom. Not to talk to, though. "I mean," she would eventually explain to the police and anyone else who'd listen, "the *look* on his *face*. You know? I mean like *strange*."

A few hours later, Jason and Beth Wesley were lying on their backs in a secluded part of the Arnold Arboretum. Against the chill, they had sandwiched themselves between two old blankets. Heads pillowed on heaped up leaves, mouths and hands urgent, they were warm enough.

They liked to come together, Jason spurting into her fist, while she closed in soft spasms around his fingers. Best was to keep your eyes open, lifting them slowly up the trunk of a giant hemlock, up and up until the moment of climax.

They had met last summer, at the Richmond Street Pentecostal Fellowship, not long after Jason and his mother had fled to Brookline and been saved. Beth was three years older. An older woman. She was almost two inches taller than Jason and some twenty pounds heavier. To be with her like this, Jason had buried some truths: that they were fornicators; that a working woman normally does not choose a boy still in high school. And what if Beth or her father found out about the cars he'd boosted, the shootout in the liquor store? Would they, as the Bible instructed, forgive seventy-times-seven? Jason found complete trust beyond his reach, adding to his existing burdens the serious sin of Doubt.

Dr. Wesley, a dentist, was an elder at the Fellowship. Beth ran his office, did the books, and was trying to become a hygienist. Because of Dr. Wesley's commitment to charity patients, there was no money to send Beth to school. She practiced on relatives. Jason had not yet offered his own jaws. Every time he thought about it, the basic weirdness stopped him cold.

Beth was slave labor, no doubt about it. Dr. Wesley paid her fifteen dollars a week.

Finances had led them to the Arboretum, which was free, for their dates. Jason's father, in remote Albuquerque, drank. He could not be trusted to pay for college, divorce decree or no. Everything Jason earned as a Stop & Shop bagger had to go straight into the bank.

Beth often bugged him about his job. Surely someone with straight A's in math should at least be a checker. But Jason was afraid the store would run a security check because he'd be handling money. His parole counselor at the Department of Youth Services couldn't swear they wouldn't ask for his previous address and discover what kind of life he'd led before he'd been saved.

Although he'd been born humorless and made more earnest still by salvation, Jason was not entirely insensitive to the irony of it. Numbers sang and danced for him; most of the checkers he bagged for couldn't even make change without the help of their registers.

He was less aware of another irony. If he and Beth were not saving money for charity and college, two universally recognized goods, they would go to movies and concerts and thus have less opportunity to do something bad. To be fornicators. But what a mystery life was! Because the more they sinned, defiling their bodies—was not the body the Temple of the Holy Spirit?—the more totally their souls flew up, like comets, wild and strong, racing past the hemlocks' sun-shot tips, thrusting ever higher until they reached the very gates of heaven. G—d's very heaven!

They'd finished. "I love you, Jason," sighed Beth.

"Me too."

She rolled to her side, propping her head for a better look at him. "You really finessed those old C.A.T.s, didn't you?"

"Only with His help, Beth."

Admonished, she hid her face against his chest. She could hear his heart, beating out the fleeing moments she had left with him. There was never enough time, never. He had to work, or study, or go off to one of those twice-weekly appointments he was so secretive about. And of course next September he'd have to go to college.

If tomorrow weren't Sunday, when she could be sure of being near him for a least the two hours Fellowship lasted, Beth would die. Right this minute, of longing and loneliness.

Chapter 2

The following Tuesday, one hundred and thirty-six English teachers, the real people Miss Touhey had said would be reading the essays, began setting forth. Drawn from every part of America, they would sleep that night at the Beasley Center, a converted mansion set in the horse country north of Boston. The Scoring would begin Wednesday morning.

Dodge Hackett, on a year's leave of absence from the high school where he normally taught upper-level English, watched O'Hare airport drop from view. This would be his fourth Scoring; imagining the reunions ahead, his pleasure was tinged with something like stage fright. He valued this feeling, believing that it proved he was doing something worthy, significant. The day he stood before a new class without its bracing reinforcement would be the day he'd quit teaching.

"Hackett," mused his seatmate, a Winnetka businessman whose own name Dodge had failed to catch. "Sounds familiar to me. Did you have one of my daughters?"

The old Dodge would have mentally riposted, Have her, sir? Do you seriously expect me to confess it? But events had finished him for that kind of joking, even to himself. Especially to himself.

The businessman was probably remembering his name from the news coverage of Courtney's suicide. Dodge had no intention of getting into this. To change the subject he started explaining about the Scoring.

"It's fun. Cross between a cruise ship and summer camp. An enclosed environment where everything's done for you. Meals and snacks on schedule, maid to pick up your room. One required activity, reading. We get more of that than we want. Much more."

"How many essays do you handle?"

"In all? Eighty, ninety thousand."

"What's your share?"

"I never counted. It's five days. Hundred and fifty a day, maybe? You have to keep a decent pace or they don't ask you back."

"Think they're fair? The C.A.T.s?"

The man's question was polite rather than urgent. His own daughters, he'd already told Dodge, thrived on academic pressure. They'd taken the C.A.T.s in stride, landing safely in their first-choice colleges. Which, he'd added, was only right, considering the astronomical school tax he paid.

"Fair as they can be. Every essay gets two different readers. If the computer says their scores are too far apart, a Master Reader steps in to settle it."

"So the computer sets the scoring standard?"

"No. That's all done before people like me climb aboard. The kids write their essays on Saturday. They're immediately bundled up and expressed to the Beasley Center for the Scoring. Strict security, of course. Sunday and Monday the Table Captains—experienced Readers— cull out a representative cross-section."

"From ninety thousand essays? Come on."

"I used to wonder about that too. But they use the same sampling techniques as professional polltakers. All the geopolitical variables. Coastal or heartland. Big school or small. Public or private. Rural, suburban, urban."

"Urban? They actually drop their guns and knives long enough to write something?"

A bid for North Shore solidarity. Too trite; Dodge declined it. "I guess. Anyway, the TCs, Table Captains, read like mad and locate the norms by which the rest of the essays get scored. It's a four-point scale."

"And then the computer tells you how you're doing. Big Brother."

Trite again. "Mm," said Dodge.

"Well. Doesn't sound like much fun to me. But you better enjoy it while it lasts. Japs're probably inventing a reading machine right this minute."

Relishing his wit, he flipped open his *Forbes*.

Under his cavalry mustache, Dodge's smile was benign. To communicate certain key charms of the Beasley Center would require details he was unwilling to divulge to a stranger whose taxes paid his salary. Parents tended to be strongly invested in the notion that public school teachers had zero sex life.

Stretching out his legs as well as the cramped space allowed, Dodge raised them slightly for the benefit of his stomach muscles. He was not on friendly terms with these legs. If they were correctly proportionate to his long waist, he'd be six-one or two instead of a bit shy of five-ten. There was also the matter of his hair. Straight and brown, it lay flat against his skull, giving him only two choices: straight bangs or slanted. Allison, the woman he'd been seeing until Courtney killed herself, had experimented with various conditioners. "It's hopeless," she had despaired eventually. "Too limp. You'll have to get a body perm."

Height and hair aside, he felt terrific. He'd spent the fall bicycling to California and then up the coast. The entire width of Kansas, a fierce headwind had slowed him to four laborious miles an hour. The struggle and tedium had quite literally blown his mind, leaving it stunned, purged. He was still in this condition when he reached the Rockies. Midway through a particularly toilsome climb, he dismounted, his breath tearing craters in his chest, his legs rubber. Head tipped back to sip some of his precious water, he saw, as if for the first time, his surroundings. The wide, radiant bowl of blue overhead! The crisp elegance of the snowcaps that edged it! A crazy joy leaped out of his parched and aching throat.

Later, calmer, he knew he'd been given the starting point he'd half-consciously been groping for. Beauty existed, permanent and real, a clean solid plank across the bog he'd been trapped in since Courtney's death. Standing on such a plank, knowing its solidity, a man could dare to begin afresh.

His stomach exercises finished, the businessman exhibiting no further interest in him, Dodge returned to his Elmore Leonard paperback. Behind his reading glasses— he was slightly farsighted—his brown eyes were alert. The Leonard male, the ideal of masculinity implicit in these entertaining tales, seemed worthy of study and, possibly, emulation. Unfortunately, the Leonard man who knew himself best often had gained his insights at the cost of a prison term or the kind of violence you hoped never came your way.

To Dodge, self-knowledge was like money: hard to have so much you couldn't use more. He tried to live consciously and reflectively, even when contrary longings confused his head and heart. There was nothing mild or scholarly about these confusions. More than one sleepless night, exhausted by their careening racket, he'd had to cave in to Valium and the reminder that the overexamined life is not worth living either.

His major blind spot? In intimate relationships, his alertness and sensitivity operated in one direction only: out.

No less fundamentally than he sweated salt, bled red and sneezed the pollens of springtime, he was a man eager to please. Watchfully attentive to others, he kept neglecting to discover, much less to ask for, what might best please himself.

His best event, then, was the short sprint. The five-day duration of the Scoring, for instance. In and out too fast for resentment's muddy paws to catch up with him.

His buddies! In a few hours they'd be together again. Ara and Jeremy, Di and Kate. He loved them all, loved the self he became around them.

Once, rashly, he'd tried to describe to Allison the alchemy wrought upon the buddies by the temporal and spacial finitude of the Beasley Center. Since Allison wasn't in the teaching game, he'd taken pains to draw the atmosphere of the scene carefully.

When he was finished with his shipboard and summer camp analogies, his ad hocs and sui generises, his assertion that the overused and debased "unique" might, in the instance of the Scoring, actually be warranted, Allison had a question. "Why don't you call them?"

"What? Who?"

"Ara and Di and the rest. Invite them for the weekend. I'd enjoy meeting them."

"You've missed the point."

"What point?" she'd incredibly asked.

He pressed his neck against his headrest, inwardly groaning. He was at it again, marshalling new evidence against a woman who was history. Massaging stale disappointments.

It wasn't as if Allison had ever been, in Kate's phrase, tenure-track.

Ara called temporary entanglements "flavors of the month."

Just a few more hours and there they'd all be. Oh, and

Prescott Beasley, too. Humanism's Last Stand Against the Wasteland.

But he liked Prescott, so why the cynicism? Because the old man, at eighty, somehow had kept green the idealistic hopes that originally propelled Dodge into teaching? Hopes that Dodge today often found a source of rebuke or embarrassment?

His friendship with the old man had begun, as everything in those days did, with the old school tie. Prescott had been in the stands the day Dodge had been carried off the soccer field on a stretcher, his knee wrenched all to hell in the Andover game. He had visited Dodge in the infirmary and stayed lightly but kindly in touch ever since. "You're a good un," he'd say with unfailing conviction, "a *good* un."

His mother, busy with yet another marriage, never said things like that. Nor did his father, heedless in California.

Chapter 3

"Becca," Di said, trying to keep it light. "Are you really going to let me go without saying goodbye?"

Becca was. She'd found the diaphragm. Her entire life with Di was built on fraud.

She wants me to cry, Di knew. Play sinful shamefaced Eve to her avenging angel.

"Well, I'll say goodbye myself, then. See you Sunday night."

Becca met her eye. "How can you do it? I mean, how *can* you?"

But Di would no more justify herself than weep.

"Till Sunday," she said, closing the door gently behind herself.

Nice old farmhouse door, given a cruel, hinge-wrenching slam by Becca late yesterday when she found the diaphragm. Nice old farmhouse life, two nice-looking teachers—Becca, with her golden mane, was downright gorgeous—in their trim and energetic late thirties. In summer, Tanglewood's music was a half hour away. In every season, clean, sweet air. At night the stars clustered thick and brilliant; you might reach up and take one in your hand, like an apple. There were real apples too, Jonathans, and juicy little Seckel pears, from their own trees.

They were tolerant of each other's newspaper, book and magazine mess, compatibly strict about bathroom scuzz and kitchen grease. Best of all, Di was convinced that no one, out here in the unworldly boonies, ever wondered what happened in their beds.

On the downside, Becca periodically drank too much. And now a second worm revealed: Di annually fucks Ara.

"If I've put up with your drinking all these years," she'd shot back at one point, "you can damn well put up with Ara."

When she was sure Becca wasn't going to come running from the house repentant, Di put her car in drive.

There was decent bus service to Boston, but she always drove. The Beasley Center reimbursed mileage and tolls, and you never knew when you might need an escape hatch.

Especially with dirtbag Marilyn Milledge there.

Poor Becca, suffering silently ever since Milledge had blabbed at that Women's Studies workshop in October. Well, hardly silently. Tearass mad drunk, and, being

Becca, rampaging through every grievance but the one that was breaking her heart.

The workshop had been followed by a three-day weekend—Columbus Day. Becca had stayed drunk until late Monday, going off Tuesday morning with trembling hands, a face like death, and no guarantees she could stay sober through lunch hour. Milledge had a lot to answer for.

Though not as Becca saw it. In the uproar that followed yesterday's revelation of the diaphragm, Becca had kept insisting the woman had intended no malice. At the workshop, Becca and Milledge had been on the same panel, Deconstruction and Feminism or some such. At lunch afterwards, Milledge mentioned knowing Di from the C.A.T. Scoring. Were she and Becca friends?

"Mohawk's a small faculty," Becca had replied. "We say hello, pass the time of day."

Evasions like this were an old story. Becca loved to play fly on the wall. She was unable to resist an unguarded diary or personal letter.

She'd lied, then, about living with Di, and received, in return, a report on Di and Ara. The core outrage, Milledge had claimed, was the psychological damage being done to Ara's three daughters. "Can't you see, Di?" Becca had parroted tearfully. "Our fathers are the first men we know intimately. Their model of maleness will influence every subsequent response we make to men. We have a collective responsibility to keep fathers honest! How can we rid ourselves of pests unless we cut off their food supply!"

Di, according to Becca, was the sole sinner. Milledge, who'd passed the C.A.T. gossip off as fact, she considered motivated solely by high-minded principle. Her own lying and rooting through Di's half-packed suitcase she refused to discuss.

Di's hands clenched on the steering wheel. Unfair! *Unfair!* The tears Becca had been denied now poured freely.

A horn, punitive, blasted at her for being out of lane. She gave her eyes an angry swipe. What am I, killing myself over a liar and a dirtbag?

And to think that at last year's Scoring, when Kate had complained about having Milledge as a roommate, she, Di, had defended the creature. "So she's kind of gross. Becoming America's major Feminist Literary Theorist has to take a toll someplace. Chalk it up to the cause."

Furious as she was, at the thought of Kate, Di had to smile. Kate should be able to help cook up some way to get even with Ms. Femlit. Except then Kate will know more about my business than I want her to. Ara too. And the whole C.A.T. gang.

Is this my year to come out to them?

If not you, who? If not now, when?

How quaint the old challenge sounded. Her answers, though, still seemed as fresh to her as a Berkshire morning: anyone else; never. She would not be categorized and pigeonholed to serve other people's stupid needs for such definitions. She would *not*.

Chapter 4

Dodge grabbed his suitcase from the carousel and, following the instructions he'd received in the mail, made his way to where he would find a chartered bus. The bus would run all evening, collecting incoming Readers and bringing them to the Beasley Center.

His waiting colleagues, clustering around a Center staffer who held a C.A.T. placard, were easy to spot. Every edge—the heels of shoes, the bend of elbow, shoulder or knee, revealed a telltale blur, sag, softness. Women tended to wear their hair whatever way it grew and in its own color. The men's longish cuts bespoke frugality more than fashion. Mouths were unguarded. Eyes, often helped by glasses, readily lit up at the mention of a favorite book or poem.

Around them streamed a completely different breed— pinstriped passengers from the New York shuttle. Not a soft edge in the lot. Whatever their depletions from a business day in Manhattan, they strode through the terminal as if they owned it, their leather heels authoritative against the terazzo floor.

Among the teachers, Dodge spotted several familiar faces. Not wanting to join the group until he had remembered their names, he lingered out of sight next to a pillar. From this vantage, he could observe what happened whenever a pinstriper allowed his or her attention to be snagged by the C.A.T. placard. It packed, Dodge happily noted, a certain punch. Passersby young and close to their own test memories winced and rolled their eyes heavenward. Anyone old enough to have teenagers tested this year looked abruptly sandbagged: This too? On top of the LBO, the IPO, the Dow, I have to deal with this?

Dodge loved it. We're rumpled, we sag at the seat, our annual salary you call a month's pay. But unless we say so, your kid doesn't get in his first-choice college. Got that?

Before his memory bank could release the names he'd been waiting for, the bus arrived.

"Dodger! Nick of time, my man."

"Nice to see you again."

Frank St. Leger he remembered as the tall stooped man swung into the aisle seat next to him. A peripheral.

Frank taught at Carleton College, in Minnesota. They were in the throes of core curriculum change, and Frank wanted Dodge to know every detail. Giving him half an ear, Dodge started thinking about roommates, wondering who he was going to get this year.

There were no single rooms at the Center. If you had made a friend during a previous Scoring, you could ask to be put together. Otherwise the Center's administration would make a match based on age, feelings about smoking and other, less obvious, variables. Rumor had it that special care was taken to never match up college teachers inclined to academic snobbishness and high school teachers inclined to defensiveness.

Dodge had never yet requested a roommate. The buddies were otherwise committed.

Ara's perennial roommate was, in fact, one of the familiar faces he'd recognized in the group waiting for the bus. Arthur Ring was his name. Dull but obliging, Arthur could be counted on to get lost while Ara and Di were in Ara's bed. Jeremy, the third buddy, would room only with other blacks, a principle also followed by the rest of the black Readers. "They've got to ask some of us," Jeremy had explained. "Can't have a modicum of fairness without *some* of us. Problem is, bright black kids don't dream of becoming English teachers. Specially bright black males. C.A.T.s wants black men at the Scoring, they have to hustle, look some. We agree to sleep with whites, we be too easy on them."

The last buddy, Kate, was of course out of the question because girls roomed with girls at the Center, boys with boys. Officially, sex among Readers did not exist. Officially, the setup did not offer enough privacy.

Four years ago, Kate and Dodge had been tablemates and then, the final evening, lovers for two stolen and wildly abandoned hours. The next morning, sitting next to Kate in the silent scoring room, Dodge had to struggle with erection and inattention. "Me too," she'd giggled at coffee break. "Like being eighteen again," said Dodge. She'd frowned, suddenly serious. "At eighteen," she said, "I knew nothing." Dodge grinned at her. "Amazing how people change." But she, gone inward, had refused to play further.

The following year she'd cut short his eager greetings. "I'm off the screw-around list," she said. "That guy I'd been living with? Rob? We got married in February." Dodge, shocked by how gypped this news made him feel, summoned congratulations. "It's your doing," Kate said, enjoying herself. "Before you, Rob was the only one I'd ever, you know, had orgasms with. I wouldn't dare marry under those circumstances." "Fine, but why pick Rob? Why not me?" "Courtly, Dodge. Very courtly. But give me a break. Rob wanted to get married. You didn't."

One nice thing though: having been his lover, however briefly, Kate now seemed a close and dear friend. Much closer and dearer than the small sum of their hours together warranted—though of course you had to factor in the special intensity of the Scoring, the way the hermetic quality of the Center distorted time.

Dodge's fantasy was that the Center would decide to allow men and women, himself and Kate, to room together. Kate loved his backrubs—taking herself off the screw-around list had not precluded backrubs. Door locked, teeth brushed, in their jammies, nicely stoked with booze, both of them relaxed from laughing with the other buddies, Rob far away in Chapel Hill, Dodge would say, What about a little rubdown? Anything could happen, anything.

The bus was being slowed by thickening traffic along Route 1. Frank St. Leger had abandoned curriculum issues to start complaining about the highway, a squalid blur of fast food outlets and retail strip. "Who supports all this stuff? Look, another carpet showroom. Must be the fifth one I've seen tonight. How many carpets does the normal person need?"

"I've heard that carpet-mania is directly related to the food supply. An additive in the burgers and tacos."

Barking his odd, two-note laugh, Frank quoted Robinson Jeffers: "Shine, perishing republic."

See? Dodge trumpeted to his mother's latest husband and every other disdainer of the teaching profession. Even guys like Frank St. Leger can come up with good lines. Never underestimate literature's saving grace.

The bus now swung onto a lesser highway. Within fifteen minutes they had reached the tranquil pastures and estates of Madison, the town in which the Beasley Center was based. "All *right*," Frank brayed as they passed an imposing Georgian pile. "More like it, huh, Dodger?"

Having grown up in a house no less grand, Dodge knew that aristocratic surroundings hardly guarantee an aristocracy of mind. Probably, though, he and the other Readers belonged here, surrounded by Madison's spacious, ordered beauty, far more than they belonged to the highway strip.

If America ever came to its senses, teachers would be paid enough to buy houses in America's Madisons.

This sentiment would please Frank. But Frank, no intimate, did not activate Dodge's impulse to please. Frank was a leech, not to be encouraged. Five days in the wrong company could get murderous.

Chapter 5

The Beasley Center stood on land granted to the first New World Beasley by King James II of England. Before the founding of the town of Madison, then, there had been Beasleys in these parts.

The family grew and branched, sending its sons into profitable enterprises like the China Trade and, subsequently, investment in textile mills and shoe manufacturing. In the last quarter of the nineteenth century, the Beasley birthrate dropped precipitously, with the result that the wealth of previous generations began to funnel toward a single man, Prescott Beasley's spendthrift grandfather. It was he who had torn down the "perfectly good" rambling clapboard house that had sheltered so many generations. In its place, he had commissioned Richard Morris Hunt, Newport's darling, to design the Italianate villa that was now headquarters for the corporation that managed the C.A.T.s and their related offshoots.

The essays were scored in the gilded ballroom where Prescott's various aunts had endured their coming-out parties—lavish affairs that had led, in every case, to adamant spinsterhood. To house the Readers and provide them with a lounge, an indoor lap pool, and an exercise room, two vast wings had been constructed. Extending from the rear, these motel-like additions did not entirely spoil the villa's appearance. Even so, anyone approaching along the long, curving drive would know that times had changed.

And changed some more, Dodge noted to himself as the bus came to a stop under the majestic porte-cochere. Hedges and shrubberies were either overgrown or dead and tangled with weed vines. Paint that had needed touching up four years ago, when he'd first come here, now hung in long flakes that reminded him of shagbark hickory. The crystal chandelier and sconces of the main hall were dusty, gray with dead light bulbs. The green and white marble floor was sadly scuffed.

Hard times. Last year the pool's filter system had broken down. Witnessing these further examples of decay, Dodge doubted the money had been found to fix it. Prescott's principles in action: one, the Beasley land must remain intact; two, raising the test fee would hurt America's poor, shut them out. "What's five bucks, is the board's attitude," Prescott had confided to Dodge the year before. "My first salary, I told them. They thought I meant hourly. Dropped their socks when I said it was five a week. They think I'm a dinosaur but they don't dare say so. Just because I'm retired doesn't mean I can't change my will. Leave the whole works to a dog and cat hospital or some such."

Dinner, the first night of the Scoring, was traditionally a cold buffet. The kitchen, too, had declined in quality, but even in the days of interesting food, only wimps and misfits ate on arrival. Everyone else moseyed around the lounge, savoring the intricacies of shakedown. The bar, thank God, was still run on a nonprofit basis.

First, though, came check-in. Dodge picked up the envelope that held his room assignment, name tag, key, schedule, and the all-important alphabetical list of Readers. What he called stagefright swept him freshly; now he would know for sure who had made the cut and who hadn't. Cheatham, Jeremy. Naturally. (Jeremy would be the first to add that "naturally." Because he was overly race-conscious himself? To anticipate the racism of his white listener? Dodge had never decided.) Royce, Diane. Savitch, Katherine, Stepanian, Ara.

All buddies present and accounted for, he had just begun to scan the rest of the names when Frank St. Leger's happy cry interrupted. "Hey! Dodger! Guess who's your bunkmate?"

Double bourbon in hand, Frank tagging behind, Dodge made his way through the crowded lounge. In the buddies' usual corner he found Ara and Jeremy.

Ara, corkscrew curls grayer this year, had a merry face dominated by quick Chinese eyes, a fleshy nose and a Cossack mustache. After finishing his degree, he'd knocked around the heavy lifting world until he had produced his first book, short stories that were a resounding critical success. A second collection, no less admired, landed him his present tenure, head of Creative Writing at Washington University in St. Louis. Two of his three daughters, the girls Marilyn Milledge had worried to Becca about, had inherited his looks. "The middle one," he'd say in his cups, "is beautiful and depressive. Like her mother."

The corners of his wiseguy mouth, even in repose, tweaked upward. He had a huge white smile. Exchanging an elbow-locked hug-with-handshake with him, Dodge felt quite tall.

Jeremy, too, could make people laugh, but Jeremy's looks had nothing of the jester about them. "I had hate at first sight with Jeremy," Kate had once told Dodge. "Then I realized I was inventing flaws so I could presume, slob that I am, to breathe the same air."

Another hug-with-handshake. Jeremy's elbows were

slightly looser than Ara's. Dodge easing up his own, the two men's chests actually touched. Jeremy was as handsome as ever, wearing, this year, his hair trimmed closer, his mustache thicker and broader.

It was their mustaches that had originally brought the three together. The question had arisen at the bar: Undeniably, Ara's was Cossack, Dodge's cavalry. But what should Jeremy's be called? "It's a Menjou," Ara had insisted. "No, no," said Dodge. "Much more riverboat gambler. An abbreviated Gable." "*I* call it my wife's idea," said Jeremy. Di, amused, had to butt in. "Swear," she'd implored the handsome stranger, "swear you'll never shave it." "Ah," Ara had leered by way of introducing himself, "you like mustaches?" He and Di had slid between the sheets the very next night, Kate had later informed Dodge.

Jeremy was the head of Freshman-Sophomore English at Michigan State. His wife had an important job in state government, which he described as "steel brushes in both hands, salvaging Rust Belt industry." In *his* cups, Jeremy had once said that he and his wife were putting off children until they were positive they could handle the long haul. "Fatherless children of color are thick on the ground. Don't have to make your own."

Unlike every other black professional Dodge had ever known, Jeremy cared nothing for clothes. Tonight he wore ancient Levis, a ravelled tee shirt, and a somewhat stained V-necked sweater that might have been new when he was in college. Ara was dressed exactly like Dodge and Frank—ironed chinos, shirt fresh from its laundry cardboard, tweed jacket.

Aside from letting Frank shoulder in and shake hands, no one paid much attention to him. By now Dodge was convinced the man had asked to room with him. Not for

23

himself, which would be bad enough, but to insinuate himself into the buddies' charmed circle.

The buddies were a recognized group, one of five or six. The existence of these groups supplied the Scoring with a vital undercurrent, though it was, of course, bad form to appear overly cliquish. Ara liked to talk about the lip service paid to collegial openness, the real game being who was in and who was not and what they were doing about it. Central to his theory was that no genuinely popular kid could possibly end up as an English teacher. "Popular kids don't have time to read," he'd declared. "They also lack motive. Why seek out imaginary worlds when the real one's so complete? Better face it: we were semi-popular. At best."

"I'm still semi-popular," Kate had admitted. "Everywhere but here. Here, for some reason, I'm popular."

The buddies had nodded. Kate had spoken for them all. And because they were popular, peripheral Frank had maneuvered hungrily into their midst.

"Oh, hey," he was now saying, "I thought of a new déjà vu for you guys."

"Déjà vu all over again," had been invented last year. "Shrimp scampi," Dodge remembered, had been listed on the dinner menu, starting everything. Someone mentioned "soup of the day du jour," followed in quick progression by "pizza pie," "rice pilaf," "gelato ice cream," and "demitasse cup." Then on to constructions like "Are you taking the le Car, dear?" to (Kate's contribution near the end of the uproarious meal) a cosmetic company that sold "fango active mud." By then the rules of the game had shifted so that you scored highest if no one got it, and no one but Kate knew that fango was Italian for mud. Her triumph, however, was almost instantly capped by a matched set from Ara: "the la Brea Tar Pits."

Frank must have been sitting at their table that night.

Ara's eyes, swinging toward him, went ultraChinese. "Yes?"

"DC current," said Frank.

Mmph, the buddies said. Yeah. Ha.

No one, Dodge saw, really laughed except Frank. DC current. Not bad. But déjà vu was last year's game, yesterday's paper.

"Hi, men."

It was Kate. Warm, full-breasted hugs for the buddies, a look and a handshake for Frank. Kate was in one of her gypsy outfits, full-sleeved white blouse, embroidered vest, a skirt with a bright border, boots that looked expensive. Her streaky blond hair hung down her back in a thick braid.

"Regard," she announced, spreading her arms wide, "a happy woman. The roommate god has hurled his thunderbolt elsewhere. I got nice little Naomi Fishbein and some other poor soul will suffer Marilyn Milledge. Where's Di? Oh wait. Oh *shit*. What if *Di* got the Milledge?"

Where the hell was Di? The dining hall was emptying fast. The buddies had finished eating and were pouring themselves coffee, waiting for their inexplicably missing member. At the next table sat Chief Master Reader Cliff Rasene with his coterie, their proximity dampening. Frank's presence, too, had taken a toll.

Suddenly and theatrically, Kate caught her breath.

They swiveled around to see. Di was entering the hall just as Marilyn Milledge was leaving.

From the back, Marilyn appeared constructed of two triangles, one formed by her exuberant orange hair, the other by a tentlike dress, also orange, that fell in fine pleats nearly to the floor.

When someone so physically imposing, and a Table

Captain besides, stops to say hello, you respond. Di kept moving, a snub both absolute and obvious.

As Di came closer, her friends could see that her un-smiling mouth—she always wore bright red lipstick—seemed pasted onto her set, white face. Her gray eyes looked smudgy, her black knit dress hung waiflike from hunched shoulders. Only her dark hair, cut in the sleek bob she'd copied from Louise Brooks, was normal.

Ara rose, guided her into a chair. Sitting beside her, he reached around to offer—Rasene was watching—a brotherly hug.

Di heaved an enormous sigh and buried her face in her lover's neck. She's inhaling him, Dodge knew, she's finding him again in his smell. Whatever had hunched her up, it wasn't Ara.

"Drink," Ara soothed, curling her fingers around the last of his Scotch.

Di downed the watery stuff in two gulps. Leaning back, she gave the table a wan smile. "A cop caught me speeding. I was practically at the Center's gate."

"Poor baby," said Ara. "You get a ticket?"

"Thirty dollars."

Dodge and Jeremy caught eyes. Jeremy shrugged. He didn't get it either. So much woe? Over thirty dollars?

"Thing is," Di went on, "the cop was a woman. Young. Had one of those hot-potato accents."

"Oh," said Kate. "You tried to talk yourself out of the ticket. Sister to sister."

But Di shook her head, her eyes filling.

Ara passed her his handkerchief.

"Jesus," she said, after blowing her nose. "What a basket case. Sorry, everybody."

Rasene's table was frankly staring.

Kate stood. "Sustenance-time, Di. I'll do you some food and Frank will run to the bar. Double Scotch on the rocks, Frank. Dodge, you change the subject. Tell Di about your bicycle trip.''

Chapter 6

Shortly after sunrise, Dodge was out testing his latest indulgence, a pair of roller skates with all four wheels set in a single row.

He stroked his way out of the parking area and down the main drive. Dew sparkled on the rough-cut grass. Going to be a glorious day.

A smaller driveway branched to the right. Here, under sheltering evergreens, the paving was wet, strewn with slippery needles and twigs. Avoiding the worst patches, he climbed a short rise and then sailed down to the turnaround in front of the cottage Prescott Beasley had built himself when he'd willed the villa to the Center.

As Dodge had hoped, Prescott was up and out, supervising the morning routines of Butter, his ancient golden retriever.

Butter was named less for his color than the form his sociability took. Rejuvenated by Dodge's company, he practically butted him off his skates. "I'm distracting him from his business," Dodge apologized, trying to pat the dog while shaking his master's hand.

"He's done," said Prescott. "Anyway, at our age there's no such thing as a distraction."

"You look terrific, Prescott."

27

"So do you. Tell me about those skates."

"They're better for my knees than jogging."

"Only that? They *look* like damn fine fun."

"They are. Want a try?"

"Not today." Prescott grinned, then became uncharacteristically shy. "How do you like the topic this year?"

Dodge knew that his old friend's retirement had been selective. Administrative quotidia shifted onto younger shoulders, he had kept the parts that were fun, like setting policy and brainstorming the annual essay topic. "It seems fine," Dodge said. "A good choice."

Prescott laughed. "Tell me that after you've been reading a couple three days and I'll know I'm hearing more than manners. Not that I have any objection to manners. Your students have anything to say about the topic? Any of them recognize the source?"

"I'm on leave this year, so I can't answer that. I'll listen around. See what the other teachers have to say."

"On leave? Nothing wrong, I hope."

A girl needed help and I ran scared. But Prescott looked so frail, his eggshell skull almost visible under fearfully stretched skin. Too old—too thin-skinned!—to burden with these griefs. "Mild burnout. I'll be fine."

"Course you will. You're a good un."

"I'm glad you think so."

They smiled at each other.

"Bad to stop in the middle of a workout, Dodge."

"Right. What *is* the source?"

"Say again?"

"The source of the topic."

"Rousseau. *The Social Contract.* Course, we had to unisex it. What, you didn't know 'unisex' is a verb? Neither did I. Got it from one of your colleagues."

"I'm ashamed of my colleague and ashamed I don't know Rousseau better. Which doesn't mean I won't show off to the others. See you soon. Tomorrow morning, if these things don't give me a charley horse." The dog was energetically nosing his skates. "*Yes*, Butter. Those are *wheels*. Want to hold him, Prescott? So he won't try racing me?"

"Butter and I have a deal. I don't interfere with his chasing, and he doesn't fuss me on my drinking."

The dog kept pace for nearly ten yards before his tubby body remembered itself and plopped to a skidding halt. Dodge gave his head a final pat and waved back at Prescott. Out of sight of the two old fighters, he had to slow down, wipe his eyes.

Wait, though. Holding back about Courtney—wasn't that more to protect himself than Prescott? If Prescott knew the truth, would he still think Dodge Hackett was a good un? Why, if not for serious doubts about his goodness, had he been driven to take leave?

Mild burnout. He should be so lucky.

People who go in for teaching, and stick with it, are more individualist than the average employee. Teachers work in isolation from their peers. Principals or department heads wishing to visit a class in progress must first ask the teacher's permission. No parent would dream of barging in. Unless some flagrancy erupts, something so dreadful that students are emboldened to complain, what teachers do behind their closed classroom doors remains between them and their consciences.

Eccentricity, if not of the type that student radar infallibly detects as weakness and license to run amok, is widely tolerated. The best teachers, the ones students actually learn from, understand how much of their work is theatre. They know that they are star, director, and producer; the students, at best, supporting cast, at worst, audience.

English teachers, arguably, are the most individualist of all. The rules of grammar constrain them, as do the biographical facts of authors' lives and the dates of literary periods. But none of this compares to the immutable laws of science and math, the verified historical record, that teachers of other disciplines must attempt to wedge into young brains. English teachers may interpret literature as they choose, unbothered—witness the meteoric rise of Marilyn Milledge!—by the opinions of others.

A wonder, then, that Chief Master Reader Cliff Rasene could whip them all into shape every year. That he could get a hundred and thirty-six Readers and seventeen Table Captains to perform, in his favorite phrase, with near-machine capability.

Oh, there were grumbles, occasional outbreaks of resistance. These never lasted. Rasene always found a way to prevail.

Was it, though, entirely Rasene's doing? Might the near-machine have a life of its own? Might it be driven by primordial forces within the Readers themselves?

Well-traveled teachers had pronounced the ballroom, with its carved and gilded pilasters, it arched mirrors and fenestration, to have been inspired by, variously, the Petit Trianon, Syon House, and Nymphenburg. The furnishings required by the Scoring—pale green formica-topped tables; Metaltone chairs upholstered in beige plastic—were pure Holiday Inn.

Recessed lighting freckled the lush ornamental plaster of the ceiling. If a day were to turn exceptionally dark, these utilitarian fixtures were augmented by the crystal chandeliers. Dusty though they were, the gorgeous throwbacks caught late afternoon sunbeams, scattering rainbows that had cheered many a tired eye.

Dodge, like most, arrived early this first day to find his

table, number fifteen, captained by Francie Squires. Francie, chic and black, taught at San Francisco State. Back when Dodge had first noticed her, he'd asked Jeremy for details. "Husband's a big-time judge," Jeremy had said, "hence the big-time threads." Astonished by this unsuspected awareness of Jeremy's for clothes—Francie dressed beautifully, dark suits with fresh white linen or silk next to her face—Dodge pressed for more. Jeremy sighed. "Francie's OK. Probably the judge is OK too. It's just that she's like a woman lawyer in a movie. You know? Struts around, jury's minding her ass and legs instead of the evidence?" Dodge thought a moment, then took this image the distance. "Do you mean she's not overly smart?" "Can't say. Never got past the ass and legs."

Up close, Dodge noticed while saying hello, Francie looked older than he'd thought. Near fifty. The great legs running up to a neat ass, firm and high.

He found his assigned placed and sat down. "Ellie Ostergard," said the woman on his left, smiling at him. Portland High School, Maine, her name tag said. Fortyish, drip-dry hair; a mom with a career. The kind of woman who had become extinct in Winnetka. Should wrap her up and ship her there. Stand her on the commuter platform, living proof you can be a mom and a pro at the same time.

Ellie was as much a veteran as Dodge, but Robert Gorman, the man opposite, was new. Case Western Reserve, his name tag said. No older than Dodge, he had graying hair and a paunch. "I take it," he was saying, "that you people have done this before. I'm new to the form, myself."

"I'm new too," said the man on Ellie's other side, his ingratiating smile showing buck teeth. He was from Cheshire Academy, in Connecticut, an institution usually dismissed by prep insiders as a "second tier safety school."

31

Instead of accepting Blodgett's offer of common ground, Gorman left him to Ellie and gazed upward to study a chandelier.

Stacia Steiner, said the place card for the empty chair on Dodge's right. Stacia with an *ah* or an *ay*?

Farthest from the monitoring presence of TC Francie were three seasoned campaigners. Joyce Brandt, near retirement, came from Baldwin High School, on Long Island. Strict but fair, Dodge would bet; probably a diehard sentence diagrammer. Joe Callahan and Mark Agresti, like Ellie, were in their mid-forties. University of Vermont and University of Virginia. Dodge knew Callahan best. Most nights he played the piano in the lounge—singalong favorites or, in less obliging moods, dissonant rags and riffs of his own improvising.

That was Table Fifteen: lifeboat; B-57; foxhole. The C.A.T.s deliberate mix of race, color, and creed. Stacia Steiner, presumably, would be their Jew. Unless she was an unusual Jew, Table Fifteen would have no Asian or Latino. Representatives of both these groups were scarce at the Scoring, probably for different reasons. Pedagogically inclined Asians tended to gravitate toward math or science, not English. The Latino shortage, if you believed what you read in the papers, was the result of racism and elitism in the society at large. The C.A.T.s, various rights groups said, mirrored and thus supported such discrimination. Dodge, convinced of the purity and inclusiveness of Prescott's vision, thought this was hogwash. A simpler, though less exciting explanation, was that pedagogically inclined Latinos gravitated toward Spanish, not English.

Cliff Rasene, led by the prominent chin of his long bald head, moved toward the lectern at the end of the room. The Scoring was about to begin. Dodge's entire right side felt exposed, chilly.

Rasene's first words produced from the sound system a

shrill whistle, widespread clappings of hands against ears. While he fiddled, in scuttled a slight young woman with short, dark hair, wearing black leggings, black granny boots, and an oversized red sweater. Stacia Steiner, said the name tag pinned in the center of her flat-looking chest, Hunter College, New York.

The sound adjusted, Rasene's welcome flowed blandly forth. Dodge turned to give the latecomer a teacher-can't-see smile and held out his hand below table level.

She clutched rather than shook it. "I could kill my roommate," she whispered.

Behind her round, gold-rimmed glasses, her deepset eyes looked feverish. Her narrow hand had been hot too. "Who'd you get?"

"Marilyn Milledge. I could kill her."

Chapter 7

"By midday Sunday," Rasene was concluding, "We will have read more than eighty thousand essays—twice. A gargantuan task, and, for all of us, a heavy responsibility. We must endeavor to read carefully and individually. We must be sympathetic, rewarding what is on the page instead of finding fault with what the student has failed to address or achieve. We must also be empathetic. These seventeen-year-olds were asked to think clearly under great pressure. Many were burdened by the sense that their whole life was on the line."

He paused to let the poignancy of this sink in. Then, clearing his throat, he moved to the more immediate arena of their own trials and pressures. "At this point in time, I'm going to ask you to open your folders."

Before each Reader was a facsimile of the topic sentence and instructions that Jason Armbruster, the Gatsby girl, and the rest had struggled with the previous Saturday.

Human beings are born free, and everywhere they are in chains.

First, Dodge decided, I'd question born free. My chains would be greed and lust. No, scratch lust. If you're not lusty at seventeen you're in a coma. Habit and fear of failure would be easier to write about. And peer pressure.

For kids who hadn't made friends with metaphor, the thing was a killer. Pretty good for the rest, though. Gave them some scope, a paradox to chew on. Which, as Prescott had predicted earlier, did not mean that he and everyone else in the ballroom wouldn't learn to hate the short sentence's every syllable as the Scoring wore on and novelty wore thin.

The folder also held a pack of photocopies—fifty essays selected from the original sample drawn according to the polltaker's science. These fifty, in the judgment of Francie, Marilyn Milledge, and the other TCs, constituted a fair cross-section. Selections from this cross-section, read and scored publicly at intervals throughout the Scoring, would expose and stamp out wayward impulses among the Readers.

Although each of the four points of the scoring scale was adequately represented, the pack contained, naturally, more specimens from the middle than either extreme, and herein lay the main threat to a Reader's good intentions. Good papers delighted, illiterate papers saddened. But what outraged, what turned a Reader vengeful, was the banality that characterized far too many average papers. It was like a river of sludge, this banality—a thick, slow-moving flow of platitudes and sitcom philosophizing. "The middle does not shine," Dodge remembered Di Royce saying. "It is dross. The Golden Mean is an oxymoron."

"Please remove," Rasene instructed, "the first eight papers, marked A through H on the top righthand corner. These essays exemplify the four points of the scoring scale. They will serve, throughout the Scoring, as the models against which every other paper can be measured. It is important to remember that while this model group *covers* the full scale, there are not *necessarily* two papers for each point."

Every test, thought Dodge, turns on its little trick. School teaches us to spot the trick. School teaches mistrust and cunning.

"Note that these eight papers," Rasene continued, "as presently arranged, are not, repeat not, in any particular order.

"You are to read the papers through once. Then, re-reading as necessary, arrange them in descending order from four to one. Finally, award each essay the score you think it deserves."

After initial rustlings, the silence in the ballroom grew profound. The Readers, as a body, might never again read with such care and concentration. And why not? When judges set themselves up to be judged, they want every possible advantage.

"Does anyone," Rasene finally asked, "need more time?"

Yes, the urgent chorus went up, *yes*. As if time were all that separated them from Solomon.

No one at Dodge's table had cried for more time. Eight fast readers, including Stacia.

In an undertone, Dodge asked her how to pronounce

her name. "As in nosh," she said. "I changed it from Stacey."

"How come?"

"Too Jewish."

His laugh came so fast he popped his ears smothering it.

The dread reckoning could be postponed no longer. "Paper A," Rasene announced. "Fours?"

In the center of the room, a hand. Two others near the back.

"Threes?"

A scattering.

"Twos?"

A forest.

"Ones?"

No ones. Disregarding the poor jerks who'd given Paper A top marks, Rasene complimented them. Paper A, in the opinion of the TCs, was "a solid two."

"Paper B," said Rasene. "Fours?"

Three-quarters of the room lifted them high.

"Threes?"

The rest responded. No twos or ones. Again Rasene complimented them. His goal of near-machine capability seemed well within reach.

"That one was really too easy," said Ellie, who'd raised her hand at four.

"Oh?" said Gorman. "I gave it a three. The idea's clever, but what about the organization?"

Ellie shrugged. "Kid seems to know what a paragraph is. And there's a real live mind working here. Signs of life aren't that common. I've learned to value them."

And you better too, everyone heard.

"Let's save these comments," interrupted Francie, "until Cliff tallies the rest of the sample."

"Paper C," said Rasene. "Fours?"

Paper C turned out to be the bane of the Scoring, an even two/three split. The TCs had awarded it a three—"A low three," Rasene admitted, "but a three nonetheless."

Table Fifteen wouldn't hear of it. The thing was clearly a two. Clearly! "Wobbly diction," Agresti began the instant Francie permitted debate. "Peculiar sentence structure," Gorman added. "I read it four times," said Dodge, "and I still don't know what the kid's driving at." "Exactly," said Stacia. "Born free or born in chains? He's trying to have it both ways." "Plus which," said Callahan, "it's dumb." "Egregiously so," concurred Miss Brandt. "*Le mot juste*," said Ellie. Only Blodgett was silent.

But their unanimity could not budge Francie. The TCs, she kept insisting, had chosen Paper C precisely because it illustrated the depths to which an essay might sink without forfeiting upper-level status. "Let's drop it for now," she finally said. "I'm sure things will be more clear as the Scoring progresses."

At the end of this first day, Rasene and the Assistant Master Readers held, as usual, their nightly pow-wow with the TCs. At this meeting, Francie learned that difficulties related to Paper C had been widespread. Many Readers, experienced or not, were dangerously confused. Every borderline three or two sent them running to their TCs for advice.

Rasene began the pow-wow by saying that the computer had tallied an historically slow first day.

Marilyn Milledge wasn't surprised in the least. "I'm a strong woman," she informed the gathering, "but I had my hands full controlling my table. No one's happy with Paper C as a three. No one. Better face it, Cliff. An ambiguous model is worse than no model at all. The better part of valor would be to withdraw and replace."

Rasene turned dark red. If you had any balls, he had just heard Marilyn say, you'd fess up to the mistake.

"All day Sunday, Monday and Tuesday," Assistant Master Reader Betty Magowan reminded the group with heavy irony, "Paper C was a clear three. On several occasions we spoke of the obvious differences between it and Paper A, differences that said, to every one of us, 'upper level.' Today you've met a little opposition and everything's different. What's going to happen Thursday? And Friday?"

Other allies chimed in, to meet other opposition.

When the noise grew deafening, Rasene looked at his watch. Banging his fist on the table to get their attention, he announced that time was up and the pow-wow over.

"Not fair," Marilyn objected. "I say we bring it to a vote."

"Hear, hear," shouted a half-dozen others.

"Betty's right," Rasene's group yelled back. "You want to rescore today's?"

"I suggest we vote on voting," Phil Hamrick, the other Assistant Master Reader said in a loud, firm voice. "This entire debate is without precedent. Absolutely without precedent."

More noise broke out. Rasene again banged the table. "It has been suggested we vote on whether a vote on Paper C would be useful at this point in time. In favor? Opposed? Betty, Phil, you count that as I did? Thank you. The nays have it. We're adjourned."

During cocktails, the passions and resentments excited by the pow-wow began to seep out among the Readers. Looking back, people would say that this acrimony over Paper C was an early sign of the explosive trouble still to come.

Chapter 8

Commerce, in the town of Madison, was limited to a hardware store, a specialty food shop, a drugstore with soda fountain, a real estate office, a small bank, a dentist, and the Colonial Grille, small and dingy. There were also two riding academies where horses could be boarded, a large-animal vet (other animal and human patients had to travel to Ipswich or Beverly), and a garden-supply place that sold, in season, local produce.

The largest single employer was the Beasley Center. Much of the work was on the menial side—rudimentary grounds care, housekeeping, kitchen. The white collar staff included Jan Dicenzo, the Administrative Director, a bookkeeper, two secretaries and their augmenting temps, and the women who served as a combination of receptionist, telephone operator and concierge.

For this position, Mrs. Dicenzo liked to hire widows looking to boost their Social Security. For one thing, they were reliable. For another, they didn't mind being asked the same old questions over and over again, by visitors new to the area. And if excess poundage, shortness of breath, foggy eyesight or varicosities made them not too quick on the draw, so what? No one but nice people came to the Center, and nice people are patient. Or will pretend to be when given no choice.

Right around the time that Marilyn Milledge and her supporters were tangling with the Rasene faction, Mrs. Ouellette, the widow who worked the 6:00 P.M. to 1:00 A.M. shift, settled herself into the little area off the foyer that had been, in the grand old days, the Ladies' Tiring Room. It was early, more than an hour until dinner. The Readers were variously occupied with drink, fitness, or private pursuits.

Mrs. Ouellette, a little deaf and intent on the tricky cable pattern she was knitting into a blue baby sweater, didn't hear the outside door open. When the attractive blond woman who had approached the counter spoke, she jumped.

"Professor Stepanian's expecting me, but I've forgotten his room number."

"Step who?" Mrs. Ouellette asked it gaily, but the young woman only repeated the name more distinctly.

Cold fish, Mrs. Ouellette diagnosed. The difficulty of her own name had given her a hobbyist interest in other peoples'. Then she'd add, "My husband's name, God rest his soul, was the only hard thing about him."

"Here we are," she told Miss Stoneface. "Ara Stepanian. Room 33E. E for east, but I guess you know that."

Already halfway through the double doors Mrs. Ouellette had automatically gestured toward, the visitor didn't bothering answering.

"You're supposed to be wearing your name tag," Mrs. Ouellette called after her. Really. Some people. Smelled like a gin mill, too.

Jason Armbruster, wearing a dark coat, a dark scarf pulled up to his eyes, stood hidden behind one of the overgrown yews that flanked the main entrance. From this vantage, he had observed every detail of the blond's successful infiltration. She'd been the second person tonight to drive up and approach the old lady's counter. Couldn't count the first, a Fedex guy dropping off an envelope. Still, more visitors could be on their way right this minute. With each new arrival, he'd learn more about how the place worked.

It was cold up here in the country, colder than Brookline. Jason wished he'd worn his boots. He also wished he could have heard what the blond had said. And what the old lady had yelled, there at the end.

The blond had made her mad, that was clear. Still, the old lady hadn't chased after her. That was good. Because if one person could get in, so could he. And once he did—

Once he did, what? A blank. All he knew was, it had to be face to face. Face to face was the only way.

With one gloved thumb he flicked the edge of the postcard he'd been carrying in the pocket of his parka since yesterday afternoon. A fireball tore through him, leaving his armpits wet, his guts sick and weak.

Arthur Ring, Ara's roommate, had cleared out until after dinner. Ara was sluicing off shaving cream—Di's pale skin beard-burned at a touch—when he heard the knock at the door.

He wrapped a towel around his middle and opened the door so that it hid him. Passing Readers could think what they chose about a woman knocking on a man's door, but if the man is seen wearing only a towel, he's asking for censure.

After Ara recovered from finding a stranger waiting, he noticed that she was stinko. This decided him: no robe. She'd barged in, as immune to consequences as every other drunk he'd had the misfortune to encounter. The towel was more than she deserved.

Gorgeous, though. A real Brunnhilde. "Are you looking for me?"

"You're Ara Stepanian, aren't you?"

"I am. Have we met?"

"No. I'm Becca Lassiter."

"And?"

"I came to find out everything I could about you."

Minding the overlap of his towel, Ara sat on the edge of his bed and waved a hand at the room's one chair. "Fine. Not everything, though. The towel stays on."

"For God's *sake*."

"You don't like ground rules?"

"I don't like grown men acting like boys."

"I see."

She didn't take the chair. Her evaluating gaze made him wish he hadn't sat down either. "Well anyway," she conceded, "you have a good strong body. Wonderful teeth, too."

She studied him some more. Ara waited.

"Do your daughters look like you?"

"My daughters. How do you know about them?"

"People talk. Do they look like you?"

"Two do. The middle one doesn't."

"Was that last one supposed to be a boy?"

Ara showed her the palms of his hands. "My wife wanted a son. Though she might've known better."

"Why?"

"We lost our second baby. She was a girl too."

His writerly self was taking over. Caution to the winds. "The daughter who doesn't look like me is beautiful. Almost as beautiful as you. She's not happy, though. It worries me, her bottomless appetite for misery."

"What else do you worry about?"

"The usual. Nuclear holocaust, environmental collapse, getting old, getting cancer."

"You have health problems?"

Ara tapped a knuckle on the bedside table. "Not yet."

"*No* health problems?"

"What, do I look sick?"

42

"No. But you're older than I expected."

"Yeah? How's your health?"

"My health? My health is not relevant."

There was a knock on the door. "Mind getting that?" he asked.

"Who is it?"

Ara pretended he didn't know. "It's been an evening of surprises."

Another knock, louder.

"If you don't get it I will. Clearly it's someone who knows I'm in here."

Becca marched to the door and flung it wide.

For a long moment Di stood thunderstruck. Then she reached out to touch her friend's cheek. "Becca," she said, sounding if she'd nailed down something elusive and puzzling. "Ara?"

"Hi, Di. Nice to see you."

His dryness seemed to wake Di up. "Becca, what in the *world* are you doing here?"

"I wanted to meet him."

Di shut the door and moved between her two friends, looking closely into Ara's face. "What's she told you about herself?"

"Nothing."

Di weighed this.

"You know me, Di," he went on. "Patience of Job. Don't bother to tell me what's going on or anything."

Di squeezed her eyes shut and sent an explosive groan through gritted teeth. "All right," she announced. "Becca's leaving. I'll drive her to that motel out on the highway. Shut up, Becca. You're drunk and you'll do what you're told."

The motel was what they'd used before Ara had worked things out with Arthur Ring. "Wait," Ara said to Di. "Give me your car keys."

"What for?"

"So I can pick you up when you call me. How else are you going to get back?"

"Oh. Right."

She opened her bag and dashed the keys at his bed. Ara didn't think he was the one she was mad at, but her fury scared him anyway.

Becca's smile was angelic. "I'm very happy all your babies were girls. Very, very happy."

"Move," said Di, shoving her through the door.

Chapter 9

Kate, Dodge and Jeremy, sweaty from Nautilus, stood waiting for what Jeremy had just called the slowest elevators in Christendom. "Okeydoke," said Kate, having settled the evening to her own satisfaction. "Drinks in fifteen minutes, dinner at eight."

"Yes'm," said Jeremy.

"By the way," said Dodge with great casualness. "I asked someone from my table to join us."

Kate pounced. "Someone?"

"Stacia Steiner. She's new this year."

Jeremy reached out to circle an erasing thumb into Kate's frown. "How much is that doggie in the manger?" he sang.

Kate tossed her head free of him and stuck out her tongue. The elevator arrived, hiccuped, settled, opened.

Out marched Di, her face a grim mask, one hand a vise on the upper arm of a woman none of them had seen before.

"Di!" cried Kate. Neither man spoke. During Nautilus, their thoughts had strayed often and enviously toward the action presumably shaking Ara's bed. The sight of Di sprawled naked and langorous on the elevator floor they could have handled. Dressed in jumpsuit and boots, erect and purposeful, she struck them dumb.

"Later," she threw over her shoulder, strong-arming the other woman through the doors that led to the foyer.

Dodge, recovering first, stuck an arresting foot into the elevator.

"Well!" Kate breathed as the three friends rose.

"Strange," Dodge agreed.

"And what," Jeremy wondered, "might Ara be doing this very moment?"

The elevator had reached their floor, the third. "His room's right down there," Kate said. "You could knock on his door."

"I could. But I don't think I will."

"Dodge?"

"Kate?"

"Chicken," she confessed. "All right. The lounge in fifteen. I'll be the one with the quivering antennae."

It excited Jason to see the blond woman again, heading for the door in the company of a second woman. The second woman was wearing a name tag. The old bag at the desk didn't ever look up from her knitting. A good sign. People came and went here. He himself could come and go.

Wait, though. Why was the new woman getting into the driver's seat of the blonde's car?

They tore off, laying rubber. As the car passed Jason's hiding place, he thought he heard yelling.

Custody, that was the word. The new woman had the blonde in custody. Whatever else, he'd have to work it so there was no way he'd be taken in custody.

He heard footsteps, then noisy breathing. A tall, thin guy in a sweatsuit, sort of stooped-looking, passed within five feet of the concealing yew bush. Jason held his own breath until the man had gone safely indoors.

Once again, the old bag didn't look up from her knitting. Because the guy had been wearing a name tag? Between the blonde's arrival and departure, Jason had watched a dozen or more people pass through the foyer. They'd all been wearing name tags. Two, a man and a woman, had stood talking near his window, so close he could read their names and names of the high schools where they taught. For a moment, reading the woman's name, his heart had hammered ferociously. What if it was her? It wasn't, but what if?

These same name tags—plastic sleeve, printed card inside—were what they used at the Fellowship's Witnessing Convocations. Jason kept his in his top bureau drawer. Forgery would be incredibly simple. Get those press-on letters in the right size, invent a name and a high school.

No way he'd pass for a teacher, though. Too much of a babyface. He'd have to figure out something else.

He'd expected, by now, to have seen a watchman. He'd hang out another hour. No watchman by then—what would a guy in a place like this be carrying? A walkie-talkie? A gun?—he'd take a little stroll around.

When Dodge walked into the lounge, Stacia, holding a glass of white wine, was sitting at one end of a sofa. At the other end, Will Blodgett, fresh comb marks in his pale hair, was taking a pull on a can of Miller Lite.

Dodge decided that if the two of them hadn't drawn close on their own, he was under no obligation to strike a solidarity gong for Table Fifteen. "Come with me," he invited Stacia, "while I get a drink." Only when she was in motion did he speak to Blodgett. "How's it going, Will?"

Blodgett lifted his beer in jaunty toast and stayed put. Instantly Dodge liked him better. Catch Frank staying put. Only break, Frank's back couldn't handle Nautilus. Otherwise he'd be right here. Joined at the hip.

"Smooth," Stacia observed.

"What?"

"The way you unincluded our tablemate."

Dodge ordered a double Jack Daniel's with a squirt of soda. "Guys like Will are OK for lunch," he then said. "Not dinner. By dinnertime, the mind of Young America has done me in. Made me selfish. Cheers."

"To selfishness. And by me, he isn't even OK for lunch."

Dodge grinned. This was what he'd come for—these heedless plunges into candor, the potential for instant intimacy. What worked the magic was the pursuit of a common task while enduring a common tedium. And the enforced silence. Furtively sharing the kids' funny mistakes, you'd die for the freedom to comment or burst out laughing. At breaks and lunch, you fell upon each other's words, famished as long-denied lovers. Back on the job, the air between you felt full of magnets.

He couldn't wait to know Stacia better, to tell her about Di and the beautiful stranger. In the meantime, wasn't Blodgett too blank, too vanilla, to activate such a negative response? "That bad, huh?"

Stacia dropped her head in the way she had, as if truth lay woven into the carpet. By now, Dodge had begun to

47

find the small, knobby bones at the back of her neck profoundly appealing.

When she lifted her eyes again, each gold-rimmed lens mirrored light. "It's the cowed quality he has. His readiness to play victim. He didn't even fight back on Paper C. And at lunch? When we were arguing about Latinos? The one time he opened his mouth and got challenged, he acted as if we'd hit him."

Dodge nodded. She'd put her finger on a quality of Blodgett's that had bothered him too. "Trouble with victims, it's never a solo. Someone has to victimize. Not me, I stoutly declare, but I protest too much. Push the right buttons and I could run amok."

"Anyone could," said Stacia, abruptly sober.

But Dodge was in the mood only for merry, not thoughtful, candor. "On a desert island, would you rather have Blodgett or Marilyn? Factoring in what she did this morning, of course."

"That again?"

All day he'd tried to pry from her how Marilyn had made her late. "Just give me a clue," he now coaxed. "Animal, vegetable or mineral."

That this was a test moment they both understood perfectly. If she could bring herself to articulate the unspeakable, vault the decorums that had kept her evasive, it would be a sign that she was ready to entertain the possibility of further intimacies. Another couple, less acutely verbal, might begin with a touch, a tentative caress. Stacia and Dodge would begin—or balk; she was studying the carpet—here.

"OK," she at length decided. "Animal. Egregiously so, to quote Miss Brandt. Imagine sharing a bathroom with Walt Whitman. Walt grabs first go, tremendous great celebration of bodily wastes. You, if not a prude and prig, must celebrate them too. Or at least take them in stride.

Nothing human is disgusting, save human beings who would deem it so. Even so, you falter. You decide to wait for the coast, so to speak, to clear. It takes a long time—lousy ventilation in this place. Gingerly you edge in, start brushing your teeth. Back comes Walt for an encore. You flee, wait again, are made late.''

His expression made her laugh. ''Well? Did I warn you or did I warn you?''

''Yo, bro.''

It was Jeremy, resplendent in a navy and white striped shirt tucked into slacks, pleated and slightly pegged, that hung from red suspenders. The arms of a navy sweater that looked like cashmere lay stylishly knotted on his chest. Dodge, made mute by Stacia's account, seized on this distraction. ''You look terrific, Jeremy. Sharper than a serpent's tooth.''

It got a big laugh—they'd been dealing with mangled Shakespeare all day. ''My wife,'' explained Jeremy. ''She says I'm too old to look like a bum *all* the time. You're Stacia? Nice to meet you.''

Kate arrived soon after, immediately taking over. Against her fluent stream of inside jokes and references, neither man, and certainly not Stacia, could get a word in edgewise.

Jeremy hummed his doggie tune. Kate reddened and talked louder.

Dodge knew it was time for the trump he'd been saving. ''Last year,'' he interrupted, addressing Stacia, ''Kate roomed with Marilyn Milledge.''

''Oh please!'' cried Kate. ''Don't get me started.''

''This year,'' Dodge pressed on, ''Stacia has Marilyn.''

It stopped Kate cold. Seconds later, both women, laughing helplessly, were embracing, utterly lost to the rational world.

* * *

They went in to dinner when they could no longer ignore the meaningful eyeballing of Cliff Rasene. (Nothing more deleterious to near-machine capability than alcohol.) Dinner was merry, despite the serious quartet that occupied the rest of their table. In fact, the determination of these earnest souls to continue discussing educational methods in the face of their own banter made everything much funnier.

"Where's Ara?" Jeremy wondered when they'd finished eating. "Should we be worrying?"

"In the sense of starving Armenian?" Kate asked. "Uh-oh. I've just dated myself. What did your mothers say when you didn't clean up your plates? Think of the starving Biafrans?"

"Seriously," Jeremy said. "Missing meals isn't Ara's style."

"You looking for Ara?" Frank St. Leger stooped over them. "I couldn't help hearing. I saw him leave about an hour ago."

"Leave?" Kate's antennae were busy. "The Center, you mean? Was he with anyone?"

"Not to my knowledge," said Frank.

Stacia found Dodge's eye. *If teachers say things like "not to my knowledge," how can kids write any better than we saw today?*

"Frank, this is Stacia Steiner," Dodge said. "Frank and I are roommates, Stacia."

Stacia put out her hand and would have won her struggle against giggles if Kate had behaved. "I'm sorry," she finally told Frank. "We've been having this running joke about roommates."

"Oh," said Frank. Then, resilient as ever, "You guys feel like a drink? Might settle that corned beef."

Joined at the hip, thought Dodge. But Stacia had

charmed him; he was in love with the world. "Sounds good," he said, standing. "Lead on, Macduff."

"Actually, Dodger, it's 'Lay on.' "

"Dodge be knowing that," Jeremy informed Frank with chilling affability. "It be his little jest."

Chapter 10

The sprawling lounge, roughly Y-shaped, easily accommodated a variety of activities. The bar occupied the center of the Y. Each leg was furnished with comfortable sofas and chairs. Thick carpeting ran up from the floor to banquettes that defined and enclosed the seating areas. People also used to sit on the floor, but nowadays the grubbiness of the carpeting discouraged this.

The longest leg held the piano, a baby grand whose middle keys needed tuning. Joe Callahan was doing his best with "In the Still of the Night." A dozen variously musical Readers had gathered around him, making up in volume and enthusiasm what they lacked in finesse.

The buddies' usual corner was as far from the piano as you could get. They were talkers, not singers.

Kate settled herself next to Jeremy. Frank took her other side. "You and Stacia," Kate then directed Dodge, "can fetch the brandies. I want mine with lots of soda and ice. That beef was incredibly salty. Hey Frank? Want to open that window a crack? Who *are* these smoking folk? Why don't they know it's déclassé?"

Waiting at the bar, Dodge heard the song approach its high part, most of the singers dropping down to keys less demanding. One voice hung in, a clear, true soprano that yearned to know if her love was returned, if her dreams were coming true.

Stacia gaped in disbelief. The expressive phrases were pouring from the unlikely instrument of Marilyn Milledge.

The high part over, Marilyn's virtuosity inspired the other singers to a concluding diminuendo that caught every heartstring in the room.

To loud applause and cries of bravo, Marilyn acted the diva, blowing kisses and laughing.

"Is this an annual feature?" Stacia asked Dodge.

"Far as I know, she's never sung before. Good, isn't she?"

"She's amazing. Also amazingly inconsistent. Someone should tell *People* magazine. 'High Priestess of Femlit Gets Down with Schmaltz.' "

Callahan, in a rare gesture of relinquishment, offered Marilyn the songbook to pick the next number.

Suddenly, explosion. Coming from nowhere, up barged Di Royce, Commando Di in jumpsuit and boots. Her face close to Marilyn's, she said something. Then she turned on her heel.

That was all, for the remainder of the evening, anyone could absolutely swear to. One minute the star of the sing-along was leafing through Cole Porter, the next minute she lay crumpled on the floor, writhing in pain.

Di, a patch of color on each pale check, strode up to the bar. "Scotch, double, no ice."

Drink in hand, she turned, as if mildly curious, to face the commotion at the piano.

Marilyn had been helped to her feet. She was shaking her head, no, no. Someone had handed her a piece of tissue. Someone else offered an arm. She took it and tried to walk. A yelp of pain. Is it broken? people asked. Is it your foot? Your ankle? Tell us what's wrong!

No, Marilyn's head shook, no. "But can someone—"

Someone darted to her other side.

"Good. OK. OK. Slowly, now. *Ow.* No, it's OK. As long as I can—good."

Except for the color in her cheeks and a tiny tremor that agitated the surface of her whiskey, Di was impassive. The scene at the piano might be a play she had to watch for reasons of scholarly duty rather than pleasure. Her pose, leaning back on one elbow, seemed relaxed and easy.

The reaction of the others, singers and audience, interested Dodge. First they turned on Di with looks that said What's the meaning of this? What have you done? Once they crashed against Di's cool, though, once they absorbed her dispassionate observation, doubt and bewilderment began to leak in. And by the time Marilyn had hobbled into the elevator, apparently without offering any clear explanation of what had been done to her, there were shrugs, raised eyebrows, other signs of disengagement.

Callahan shuffled together his songbooks and stacked them on the piano bench. The beginning measures of "Walk Right In," jarring and peppy, were chased by still more jarring improvisations. Callahan had entered his private musical world. There might be another singalong tomorrow, but tonight's was over.

Di still hadn't spoken. "This is Stacia," said Dodge. "We're fetching the brandies." Indicating the rest of the group, he saw, for the first time, that Ara had joined them.

He asked the bartender for another brandy and soda. If Ara didn't want it, he could use it himself.

"Damn," said Stacia when Di was out of earshot. "I have to go after Marilyn. Don't I? Do the roommate thing?"

"You want to?"

"You serious?"

"So don't."

"That simple, huh?"

"Until proven otherwise. Which, in your case, will probably be tomorrow morning. Nothing like morning for stepanfetchit opportunities. Bright side, you can beat her to the bathroom."

"Tell," Kate immediately demanded, *"Tell."*

"Here's the deal," said Di. "One, I don't say a word. Or two, I tell you what I did without any whys."

"Come *on.*"

"That's it. You go for the what, you have to swear off pestering on the why. Otherwise you get zilch."

She extended her right leg as if to admire its lean length. "Great boots, aren't they? Ms. Milledge has been stomped. Had her toesies ground right into the floor. Ground into pulver, to use a charming locution I found in one of today's papers."

Her laugh, Dodge thought, had wild edges. Before therapy, his mother had laughed like that.

"Incredible," Kate marveled. "And then to just stand there and *look* at her. I mean!"

Di didn't respond.

"One must never quit the field," said Ara. "Never."

Kate pounced. "Ho. Did you put Di up to this?"

Ara's hand said halt. "Out of order, Kate. Under the rubric of why."

"I bet anything it's all because of that blonde," said Kate.

"Kate?"

"Yes Di?"

"You swore. Want me to stomp you?"

Kate's laugh failed to persuade anyone that Di was just kidding.

" 'Pulver'," mused Jeremy. "I like that. Ought to be a real word. I have a good one too. 'Affluential'."

But this foray met only silence. Even Frank was silent, despite the urgency with which he'd earlier reported that his powerwalk had been enlivened by the sight of Di and "a fantastic blonde" driving off together in the same car.

"Anyone know a good long joke?" asked Dodge.

Another silence followed this. At length Frank sat up and cleared his throat. Ara, however, cut in ahead of him.

"Once upon a time, three explorers were hacking through the uncharted wilds of the Amazonian jungle."

Normally the buddies disdained canned jokes. Sheep-brains were their natural audience; people who went in for telling them were dictators, control freaks. Right now, though, they desperately needed distraction. Ara's hapless explorers would do.

Otherwise, Dodge suddenly knew, our silence will accuse us. Everyone in this room will stand accused.

A weird thought. Accused of what?

English teachers fight with words, not fists. If Di had cause to lay Marilyn out, she should have done so rationally and verbally. Some onlookers would squirm and look away, some would be titillated. Everyone would know exactly what was happening, exactly how to behave. But physical force, crude and despised, accuses us. Lowers us. Erases the presumed exaltations of our graduate degrees.

Callahan had segued into variations on "Mack the Knife." Brecht, thought Dodge, Weimer segues into Hitler. Di's wild laugh; Ara's canned joke. Chaos or totalitarianism.

Too extreme. Also senseless. Must be the brandy he'd gulped.

Curiously, Ara's joke was also about choice. The explorers had fallen into the hands of a savage jungle tribe. The first explorer is asked by the King to pick death or Kalaka. What's Kalaka? No one will say. But nothing can be worse than death, the explorer reasons, and so the King announces it: *He chooses Kalaka!*

Great cries of delight reverberate through the jungle. First they yank out his long hairs. Then his short hairs. Then his fingernails and toenails. Then his tongue. After smashing his teeth, they start on his bones, big ones first, then the rest. Finally they fling him to the wild dogs that ceaselessly circle the village.

The King approaches the second explorer. *Death or Kalaka?*

They've had a real workout, reasons the second explorer. Maybe they're tired. Maybe they won't do such a job on me. One thing's certain, though—choosing death, I don't have any chance at all.

Once again, the King makes the crowd-pleasing announcement. *He chooses Kalaka!*

The savages go at it—the long hairs, the short hairs, the fingernails, the toenails, the teeth, the bones—with far more vigor and creative abandon than before. Clearly, the first explorer has been only a warm-up, a walk-through, a trial heat.

The second explorer flung to the dogs, the King approaches the third. *Death or Kalaka?*

You kidding, Jack? No contest. I'll take death.

"He chooses death," intoned Ara in his King voice.

"But *first*—up went Ara's delaying finger—"a little Kalaka."

Outside, crouched under the window that Kate had asked Frank to open, Jason was bewildered. Totally. He'd figured the dark-haired woman for a teacher—her name tag and all—but was she? Do teachers beat up on each other? Plus what was so funny? Why was that story a joke?

He'd have to look up that word—kalaka?—next time he was in the library.

The teachers still laughing, he crept back to where he could see into the room without being seen himself. Out where he'd been when the stooped guy had suddenly appeared at the window, scaring him shitless.

His gloved fist flew to his mouth. Curses insulted the Temple of the Holy Ghost.

He stroked the postcard in his pocket. *Ms. Milledge has been stomped.* Close as he'd been to the open window, that was all he'd heard, but it was enough.

It didn't take a mental giant. Milledge wasn't that common a name. The red-haired singer had written the scornful and blasphemous card. Her sin, Jason could tell just from seeing that evil glow on her face, was pride. Blinded by pride, she could never have graded his essay like it deserved.

Which proved that his very first instinct had been the right one—he had to get face to face with her. Alone and in private. He had to make her listen—make her feel the power of his Witness to G—d's holy grace and truth. Which casteth out pride. Whereupon, the error of her ways laid clear before her, she would gladly and thankfully raise his grade.

The Lord's mysterious ways. The dark-haired woman's anger had become his, Jason's, aid. Hurt foot and all, Ms. Milledge at least couldn't run away from him, flee his Witness.

His insides were water. He clenched his ass and began praying. Not since he'd found Jesus had his heart beat like this, shaking his entire body. He might be outside that liquor store, driving getaway. It wasn't the same, of course.

He knew that. But it felt the same, and so, desperately, he prayed.

Ms. Milledge had judged him, and judged falsely. He must not fall prey to the selfsame error. Judgment is mine, sayeth the Lord.

Hate the sin, love the sinner. He prayed for the strength to comply.

Chapter 11

"There's *Butter*. Howsa going, Butts? Huh? Howsa boy? Oh he's a good doggy. Oh yes he *is*."

Henry Bcasley, called Tank because that had been his baby pronunciation of Hank, gave the smelly old thing a final pat. "And how's Butter's Daddy?" he greeted his grandfather.

Prescott hid his irritation. The part of him that loved the old golden and cleaned up after his messes was boyish, still innocent and full of splendid hopes for the future. Tank, by referring to him as Butter's Daddy, had spoiled the moment. "Daddy" evoked not innocence and hope but reality: Prescott's disappointing and estranged sole issue, the son who had become, in turn, Tank's daddy.

How much of this sad state of affairs was Prescott's fault? All of it, according to his long-dead wife. "You're an only son who's *only* a son," she had liked to say. "Everything you do is for the sake of your parents, not your wife or child. For the dead, not the living."

Thoughts to spoil a lunch. Not that there wasn't more than enough trouble left over from last night. Cliff Rasene's telephoned report of the ruckus in the lounge had been vexingly skeletal. Prescott had hoped to get the skinny from Dodge during his morning skate, but Dodge seemed to have kept indoors, presumably to avoid the cold, squally rain.

Tank's morning call, inviting himself for lunch, suggested that he, too, had been briefed on the incident. Tank was a familiar figure in the Center's offices, appearing there first as an adorable child being groomed to take the reins from his esteemed grandfather, now, those fond hopes in ruins, as self-appointed watchdog of the hemorrhaging Beasley patrimony. This snooping, tolerated by Prescott because it might lead to Tank's ''taking a real interest,'' usually was enabled by the Center's youngest secretary. Tank was single and attractive. Young secretaries no less than esteemed grandfathers can live on hope.

Prescott showed his grandson a bottle of Rioja. ''I thought we'd try this Spanish stuff.''

Now it was Tank's turn to be irritated. Spic wine was either insipid or vinegary. He'd like to slap it right out of his grandfather's spotty old hand, watch it fly through the air and shatter on the white wall. The formerly white wall. Prescott's digs were getting as grubby as the Center. ''*Bon marché*, eh?'' he said instead.

''*Très bon marché*. But you should say *muy barato*. Since it's Spanish cheapness.''

''Actually, it's Yankee cheapness. I should've said it in Yankee.''

Prescott gave his grandson a look. ''I hope,'' he said at length, ''you don't expect that to bait me. I hope you understand why I consider thrift a virtue. I also hope you understand that your father's failure to cultivate this virtue has done neither him nor you any good whatsoever.''

"Let's eat, Gramper. I've got a meeting at three."

Prescott didn't ask what kind of meeting. Tank's business affairs bewildered him. Some new project was ever in the works, put together by a new set of associates. Presumably Tank earned enough to live on, and Prescott preferred to leave it at that.

Doris, the woman who came every morning to "do for" Prescott, set in front of each man a plate of meatloaf, carrots and mashed potatoes.

Tank's favorite food. He thanked Doris with genuine enthusiasm.

Prescott held his wineglass to the light. "Good color," he decided.

"Plenty of light comes through, I'll give you that."

When they had finished their rice pudding, Doris cleared and set the coffee tray at Tank's right.

Prescott frowned. "Doris? I'll pour, thank you."

"You drip all over the tablecloth."

"I do? All right, leave it with Tank. That's all now. Lunch was delicious. See you tomorrow."

Dealing with the coffee, Tank waited for the kitchen door to stop swinging before he spoke. "Can we talk now?"

"Oh. You've come to 'talk.' To relate, as they say. They also say 'to interface,' I believe. Have you heard that one?"

Tank ground his teeth. If not for this thing with language, his grandfather never would have dreamed up the Center in the first place. "You know what I'm going to say, Gramper. I've said it often enough before. Nothing's changed—not for the good, anyway. Now I hear you're ready to spring for a new roof on the west wing."

"It's not as if I have any choice, Tank."

"But you do! All the choice in the world! What do you

think, they're going to stop testing just because you make them relocate?''

Prescott bit back a yawn. He usually napped after lunch. The coffee had made him only jumpy, not alert. He was far too tired to try, once again, to convince Tank that dedicating your ancestral acres—your *intact* ancestral acres—to the betterment of the Republic was the very essence of happiness and satisfaction.

Besides, if the C.A.T.s moved, they might stop asking him to help with the essay topic. Picking the topic—it was the highlight of the year! A man sorely disappointed in his family, a man who has outlived most of his friends, would be a fool indeed to risk any pleasure that remained to him.

He was tired, though, tired to the bone. Devoutly he wished Tank gone. ''Dodge Hackett's been by to see me. You two knew each other at school, didn't you?''

''For the millionth time, Gramper, he was Sixth Form when I was a totally invisible Newbie. Besides, I'm not exactly drawn to teacher types.'' He laughed meaningfully. ''They're too tough for me. Too rambunctious.''

''Oh. You heard.''

''The office staff unloaded all over me. Brawling, Gramper, *brawling*. Not very Athenian.''

Prescott didn't know what bothered him more, the fact of the brawl or Tank's nasty thrust at one of his oft-stated splendid hopes—that American education, refined in the crucible of the C.A.T.s, could lead the entire globe back to the Golden Age of Greece. ''You keep trying to bait me, Tank. It's tiresome. A whole group cannot be judged by two women. Even if we were clear on exactly what happened, which we are not. Cliff Rasene tells me that the ostensibly injured party refuses to divulge details. She won't even see a doctor.''

''In the office they're worrying she'll suc.''

''We must hope she won't.'' Last night Rasene had said

the Milledge woman had accused the Center of pretended concern when what they cared about was liability. "You want to guarantee a suit?" she'd demanded of poor Rasene. "Then lay a doctor on me."

"She sounds," Prescott had observed to Rasene, "rather overwrought."

Rasene had fumbled his way toward an appraisal. "She's—embarrassed. Upset, of course. And hurt. Physically hurt, I mean. Mrs. Ouellette sent home for a cane, so she can walk. She can—perform her duties. People are rallying round. But the thing seems to have embarrassed her. Yes. I think that's basically it."

Tank was pressing ahead. "Boy, things sure were simpler in the old days, weren't they. Before all the Sixties stuff turned the place into the United Nations. The office people say that equal opportunity and the rest of that blah-blah hasn't helped the kids' writing any, either. But this latest episode—two ladies? One supposedly a famous scholar? Really, Gramper. If you can't count on the ladies to behave themselves, who can you count on?"

"Whom."

"What?"

"Whom can you count on."

Tank knew he'd struck home. The old man wouldn't stoop to correcting a grammar unless he was desperate. "Place is a tinderbox," he said.

Prescott tried to hide his trembling hands under his napkin. His tired eyes slogged around the room, searching for distraction.

As if sensing his master's distress, Butter insistently nuzzled at his bony thigh, his tail thumping the table leg. My great-grandfather's cherrywood table, Prescott thought, without knowing why.

"Take Butter out, will you? I'm going to lie down for awhile."

"OK. But think about it, OK? Think how nice it would be to wake up in the morning with no worries about the goddamn roof."

And with no worries, Prescott inwardly sighed, about brawling teachers. This new mixiness took its toll. And although he was a determined believer in the strength and potential of what Tank called the United Nations, he couldn't deny that some of its manifestations left him feeling feeble, overmatched, scared.

"All right," he told Tank.

"What was that?"

"I might."

"You don't have to *yell*, Gramper."

Chapter 12

Over in the ballroom, matters were scarcely less tense. Breakfast, coffee break and lunch had been dominated by rehashings and embroiderings of last night's disruptions—unless, of course, one of the principals was within hearing range. The buddies were probed energetically. "Why did Di do it? Oh come on, you're good friends with her, she must've said something." "What's Marilyn's story?" the buddies parried. "Marilyn," the probers said, "seems to have taken a vow of silence." "Well," the buddies shrugged, "there you are."

Back from lunch, the Readers were confronted by yet another public test of their scoring skills. Though routinely scheduled, these checks were hated. Theoretically, they served only to smoke out the wayward, to identify and correct those who had begun to judge essays according to mood or personal bias, ignoring their primary mission of near-machine capability. Emotionally, though, the public review put every Reader right on the firing line. Test-taking anxieties all the way back to kindergarten were revived and given an extra, accusatory spin: What? It's a simple four-point scale! You mean you haven't mastered it *yet?*

Was it self-generated, this extra spin? Paranoid? Or did it emanate from Rasene and the TCs? Fruitless queries. Irrelevant. No one goes into teaching unless he or she liked school. No one likes school who isn't a good student. Good students expect to succeed at tests. A failure to master a test is a failure to master self. It is *bad*, whether you are five or fifty. On this final point, Rasene, the TCs and the Readers were in complete, if not entirely conscious, agreement.

Today's test involved three essays, papers 45, 83, and 31. The Readers extracted the photocopies from their folders and began to read.

"Anyone need more time?" Rasene asked.

Supplication was general and plaintive.

"Paper 45," Rasene at length announced. "Fours?"

Five hands.

"Threes?"

Incontrovertably, paper 45 was a three.

"Paper 83. Fours?"

A small scattering.

"Threes?"

Half the ballroom.

"Twos?"

The other half. No ones.

"Paper 31."

Paper 31 was a reprise of 83, with slightly more threes than twos awarded.

Bad, very bad. They had failed once again to properly evaluate the difference between two papers and three papers. This particular test scoring had been devised to show that 83 and 31 were high twos and 45 a "good solid" three.

Rasene looked crushed. "Please discuss these test papers among yourselves," he said in a strained voice. "Please remember to refer to the model papers, especially the model twos and threes."

"He's crazy!" cried Mark Agresti at Table Fifteen. "It's that goddamned paper C that's screwing us up. Left to myself, I'd have given 83 and 31 twos."

Francie turned to Miss Brandt. "You scored them exactly right, Miss Brandt. Why don't you tell us how you did it."

Miss Brandt's face was an interesting mixture of defiance and abashedness. "I guessed what Cliff was trying to prove. Psyched out the test, as my students say."

France froze. "I'm afraid I don't see that as helpful. To anyone."

Miss Brandt hadn't been spoken to like this in forty years. "Have you been finding fault with my scoring?"

"No. But psyching out tests—what's the point?"

"The point is the model's no good!"

"It's not going to help if we lose our tempers, Miss Brandt."

" 'It's not going to *help*.' " Miss Brandt heavily mimicked. "I'm sick of hearing about help and helpfulness. And why do you keep calling me Miss? My name isn't Miss."

"I'm sorry," said Francie. "I'm sorry, Joyce."

Dead silence. Table Fifteen stared at its folders.

"OK," Francie sighed. "Let's begin again."

But it was hopeless, and they all knew it. Especially because they were dealing with the middle of the scale ("the mean mean," Ellie Ostergard muttered, "as in *Mean Streets*"), where bulged the great majority of the essays.

The murmurs swelled ominously ·throughout the ballroom: the entire Scoring was going to be flawed by this diehard insistence that Paper C was a valid and representative three.

Unpleasant as things were at Table Fifteen, TC Marilyn Milledge had a riot on her hands. Repeatedly she sent a whiff of grapeshot into the unruly mob of eight; repeatedly they ignored their flesh wounds and renewed the charge.

Finally Marilyn had to give up. "Read them and score them," she rapped out through tight lips. "Got that, everyone? Just—just read them and score them."

Cliff will pay for this, she thought. *Oh* will he pay. And then she'd fix that Royce for once and for all. Because if Royce hadn't had the nerve to attack her neither would the peasants at her table. Six of the eight nothing better than high school teachers!

This disproportion of talent, Betsy Magowan had insisted, had been the result of pure chance. Which was pure bullshit. Everyone knew that Betsy did the seating and Cliff approved it.

Marilyn's foot throbbed painfully in its slipper. She could feel the blood pooling there, heavy and hurtful, thickening in her swollen toes.

They'd pay, all right. All of them.

Despite the day's dual, possibly interactive, lines of strain, it was not entirely grim. By midafternoon Dodge had found, and showed to Stacia, some diversions. *Dressing like one likes instead of slavering over looking like everyone else does to be liked proves how an individual in our modern society of today can be in chains.* And: *Man is conceived in ignorance.* And: *Hamlets' mom kept this bottle up inside her.*

"Are you thinking what I'm thinking?" Stacia whispered at this last gem.

"Fatty Arbuckle?"

Francie had to shush their giggles.

Stacia, too, had found some leavening to share. *The starstruck lovers, Romeo and Juliet.* Also: *Humans are born free but live in chains. This opinion is supported by Oedipus Rex, Othello and my brother.*

"Keep going," she whispered.

My brother has been a wreckless driver all his life, Dodge read, and, further down the page, *Othello then epiphanizes himself in his true colors.*

Chapter 13

Jason's solution reached him in the depths of sleep—though not, he was positive, in a dream. Dreams, wet dreams especially, shaming and disgusting, wake you up. This time he'd had no sense of waking. It was more like he'd come back into his body from someplace else. A place far beyond earth's gravity, eternities away from the mattress sagging beneath his back, the streetlight-dappled ceiling overhead. He remembered warmth and radiance. He remembered soaring weightlessly. Then G—d, in pity and righteousness, had reached out and drawn him close to His bosom. And revealed unto him what he must do.

Sharp-set but not nervous, he approached Mrs. Ouellette's counter at almost exactly the same time Becca had, the evening before. The foyer was empty except for a group of three middle-aged men whose accents were of the rural south—waiting, it would pain Jason to know, for the taxi that would convey them to a place of sin on Route 1.

He carried a white bakery box tied with red and white string. His smile was winning, his posture—had he not been sent by G—d Himself?—relaxed and confident. He wore the suit and tie he'd bought for Sunday and college interviews. His white shirt was crisply starched.

A doll, Mrs. Ouellette gushed to herself, a regular little sweetheart.

"I'm Marilyn Milledge's nephew," Jason told her. "It's her birthday, and my mom asked me to bring her this cake. She would've come herself, my mom, but she's in bed with the flu."

"Oh I know. It's going around here too. Where do you live, sonny?"

"Wellesley." He was perfectly calm, sensing that the old bag had asked out of loneliness, not suspicion. She wanted company, that was all. But he had to keep moving. Marilyn Milledge could suddenly show up and then what?

"Wellesley's nice. My neighbors' daughter lives in Wellesley. Let's see—was it Pierce Street? Yes. Pierce. Do you know where that is?"

"Pierce. It sounds familiar, but I'm not sure exactly. I better get this cake to Aunt Marilyn, though. Could you help me find her?"

"Sure. I'll just buzz her room."

"Except won't that spoil the surprise? My mom really wants her to be surprised."

"You'd best go up and knock on her door, then. Her room's 14W. West wing. Through those doors, past the elevators. Course, she might be out. Around now they do their exercises and whatever.''

''If she's out, I'll just wait in the hall. Don't say anything if you see her, OK? On account of the surprise?''

Mrs. Ouellette roguishly zipped her lip. ''I just hope she didn't go out to dinner. Sometimes they do that. You don't want to wait all night!''

The heaven-sent courier smiled and thanked her. He'd made it! Everything had come to pass exactly as foretold! Not that he'd doubted. Doubt was blasphemy.

Finding no one in the hall, he offered a fervent thanksgiving. Then, his heart beating hard as the numbers on the doors approached 14W, he prayed some more, asking his Lord and Savior to give him the strength to complete his annointed task.

Di and Ara were in Ara's bed, making up for last night's interruptions.

Dodge, Kate and Jeremy were once again sweating and grunting through the Nautilus circuit. Tonight Stacia had joined them, but Stacia didn't do Nautilus. Her workout took place on one of the floor mats. When she'd first stretched her length onto its torn and greasy surface, she'd wrinkled her nose theatrically. ''This'll be Hobbesian,'' she announced. ''Nasty, brutal and short.''

She was wearing, like the rest of them, baggy sweats. Demure and concealing as they were, Dodge had to look away, so fraught was the moment with the frontiers of intimacy. Once she stopped shrinking away from the mat, though, once she began stretching and lifting in earnest, he couldn't take his eyes off her. Her skinny body, in motion, seemed strong and deliciously flexible. Lying on her side, both legs and arms raised, the arc of her body was a lilt, a levitation.

Miraculous as her movements seemed to him, on another level they were profoundly familiar, rooted in an afternoon that, without exaggeration, had changed his life. He'd been eleven, twelve at the most. He was watching Maria Bueno, the erratic Brazilian star, play in an invitational tennis tournament at his current stepfather's club. Without possessing enough language or insight to express it to himself, he had become instantly aware that Bueno's power strokes sprang not from musculature alone but from grace, coordination and soul.

It was a revelation, this unarticulated truth. Until this moment, women had come in two forms—athletic, loud and piano-legged like his stepsisters or limp, chain-smoking and neurotic like his mother. A woman, Maria Bueno had jolted him into realizing, need not sacrifice strength to grace, or grace to strength. And—amazing idea!—a woman need not be a Boston WASP.

From that point on, he'd been an alien within his tribe, a trouble to his family. They'd been relieved when he removed himself to the unknown and incomprehensible Midwcst, the bizarreness of public school teaching.

They'd hate Stacia, assuming he ever let them get a look at her. Not that he cared. But would she hate them? And hate him for carrying their genes?

Cross that bridge if and when we come to it.

Stacia even looked a little like Bueno. That Spanish, maybe Byzantine, mouth. The Empress Theodora, lusty lady, had a mouth like that. When Stacia had thrown back her head to laugh about Hamlet's mom, Dodge had seen that alluring arch of her teeth, narrower and more refined than his own flatfaced version.

He'd been drawn to such mouths before. In repose, their rather puckered lips seemed on the verge of bursting open. This bursting quality, he had decided, made poetry and passion seem perpetually imminent, boring, flat dailiness far away.

Fitness accomplished, he walked Stacia home, leaving Kate and Jeremy at the elevators. "I'll case the scene," he offered. "Maybe I can help you help Marilyn with something."

"Why would you want to do that?"

"Boy Scout? Guilty conscience?"

"Hear that?" Stacia said, outside her door. "She likes the TV on when she soaks in the tub. Likes it loud. Her second-string sensory affront. Still feel guilty?"

She stuck her key in the lock, turned it, and tried to open the door. It wouldn't budge. "I think you just locked it," said Dodge.

She tried again. With the door open, the television noise blared to the point of pain.

"I didn't do it," a young man cried. "I didn't!"

Marilyn was lying on the floor, her head propped against the pedestal of the desk so that her chin rested on her chest. Her eyes were horribly open and staring, though not at them.

The noise, the shock of Marilyn lying there, the strangeness of being screamed at by an anguished, carefully dressed kid—all this glued Dodge to the floor. Jason was out the open window and gone before he could pry himself loose.

Now Dodge was out the window too, in time to see the kid jump into a nondescript sedan—a two door something-orother, Dodge would later tell the police, a family car, not new, blue or gray, what difference does it make when I got the plate number?

He did get the plate number. Before that, he lunged for the locked door on Jason's side, painfully wrenching his hand as the car, gas pedal goosed hard, bucked backwards out of its parking space. Kid's scared, he thought. Can't remember how to handle a car.

This reasoning, fueled by primitive promptings from his

71

reptile brain, inspired him to run toward the car and leap onto its hood. Grab something, he thought, grab ahold. His dominant hand found a windshield wiper, but his wrenched fingers refused to function. This betrayal, for a crucial second, absorbed his full attention. Preoccupied, he realized too late that Jason had finished backing and was heading out of the parking lot.

What now, he thought, and then it was over. Jason slammed on the brakes. Airborne, Dodge jackknifed like someone pushed backwards into a swimming pool. His tailbone hit the macadam hard enough to bounce.

Quickly, expertly, the getaway artist reversed, swerved around his stunned tormentor, and disappeared into the night. Dodge's pain blazed hot and red. It tore up his spine and opened his mouth with a hot, red roar, pronouncing the plate numbers. Frank St. Leger, powerwalking onto the scene at just that moment, had the wit to commit what he heard to memory.

Chapter 14

Stacia pulled the blanket they'd given her more tightly around her clammy sweat clothes. The stink of the exercise mat clung like some repulsive personal fog, polluting every breath she took.

It didn't help that the woman interviewing her was so mega-WASP, so clean and startlingly attractive. Julia Trevor, Chief of Police, conformed exactly to the Madison gestalt—the aristocratic pasture lands, the intentional absence (Stacia assumed) of people like herself. Dodge, Chief Trevor had just said, would spend the night in the hospital. "They'll be watching for concussion, signs of injury to the base of the skull. Impact shocks can travel."

Injury to the base of the skull. Wasn't that what had killed Marilyn? Stacia shivered.

"You cold, Ms. Steiner?"

Steinah. The fancy accent matched the long straight legs, long straight nose, long straight blond hair braided into an equestrian club. A rich wife, you'd think, imagining children, horses, but Chief Trevor wore no wedding ring. "I'm freezing. Dying for a shower." Dying. She'd actually said dying.

"I'll try to make this snappy. The door to your room was unlocked?"

"I'm a klutz with locks, so I'm not positive. After I did whatever I did with the key it was definitely locked."

"And what about the window?"

"I opened it whenever I was spending any time there." Tell the woman why? Crack that porcelain mask into a million little pieces?

"Was it open this evening when you came in to change for exercising?"

"I've been trying to remember. The ballroom's pretty hot and stuffy, so I'd notice any major change. I didn't think, oh good, the room's nice and fresh, so probably the window wasn't wide open the way it was when we found Marilyn. But it might have been open a little. I know it was open that morning."

"Imagine opening it. Do you have to unlock it?"

"The first morning I did. After that, no. Which helps the kid, right? Because anyone could have climbed in?"

"The maids are supposed to close and lock the windows

73

when they do up the rooms. For energy conservation as well as security."

"Yes, but maids don't always do what they're supposed to."

"Let's move on to the boy. Did you notice anything abut the way he was dressed?"

"He looked nice. Suit and tie. Anchorman hair."

"Anchorman?"

"Or weatherman. Combed up and back instead of a side part. Not preppy."

"Were his clothes neat? Shirt tucked in?"

"Yes. He certainly didn't look as if he'd been wrestling with Marilyn."

"And the cake box? Was he holding the cake box?"

"I don't know. It happened so fast. He yelled that he didn't do it, and then he was out the window. But why—oh, right. If he was holding the box, he probably couldn't have shoved her so hard."

"We won't know she was shoved until the medical examiner's report."

Stacia decided to ignore the snub. "That desk she was lying against is real heavy. All the furniture in this place is. Built to last, I guess. Hit your head and curtains."

"Let's get back to what you saw and did. What happened after Mr. Hackett went out the window?"

"I ran over myself. I heard car noise but I couldn't see anything—there's that jog in the wall. I was going to jump out, but the door was open and people were peering in. In murder mysteries no one's supposed to disturb the scene of the crime, so I decided I'd better control that and get someone to call the police."

"Fine," Chief Trevor said, closing her notebook.

"That's it?"

"Is there something else you want to tell me?"

"Only that I think the kid was telling the truth. And I

bet that's why Dodge went after him—to tell him he believed him.''

"Right.''

Right. And not one more word will you get from me, Stacia vowed. "When can I have my room back?''

"The forensic team's State Police, so it's not up to me. My guess would be tomorrow noon.''

While Stacia had been protecting the scene of the crime, Di and Ara, like practically every other Reader in the west wing, had been attracted by the commotion. Di, all dewy and shiny from lovemaking, had pushed through the crowd to offer Stacia clothes, shampoo, anything she needed.

Sitting on Di's bed, toweling her wet hair, Stacia burst into a storm of tears.

"Sweetie.'' cried Di. "Do you hurt?''

Hurt. Yes. And Dodge was hurt. And Marilyn's terrible dead eyes, and that snooty cop right out of a Ralph Lauren ad, and the agony in the kid's face when he screamed that he didn't do it, poor dumb kid, all day long she'd either giggled herself silly over poor dumb kids or found herself hating them for mangling the language and literature she loved. Not that *Marilyn* hadn't mangled, but murder? Who deserved murder?

Di sat close beside her until the tears were over. "I set it up with Jan Dicenzo,'' she then said, referring to the Center's Administrative Director. "I made her understand that you needed to be with people who care about you. See the nice folding bed they brought? All made up for you? My roommate's Lily Freese. Doesn't talk, doesn't snore, salt of the earth. You'll love her. OK? Sure? Good. Now blow your nose and wash your face and we'll go find ourselves a nice strong drink. Oh, and I know just what you mean about that cop. She caught me speeding the first night. Some women give sisterhood a bad name.''

Meanwhile, Kate had found Jeremy in the lounge. "Thank God. I've been dying to ask you. That blond policeperson—ever seen her before?"

"No."

"On the elevator? With Di?"

"Not the same woman."

"But a noteworthy resemblance, you'll admit."

Jeremy shrugged.

"Come *on*, Jeremy. Why was Di so upset the first night?"

Jeremy still wasn't following.

"How," Kate asked the ceiling, "did men ever rule the world? The policeperson, Jeremy! When Di saw her, she saw her friend—*with whom she'd been fighting.*"

"Fighting? How do you know?"

"Why else would she have been so upset?"

Jeremy considered it. "Assuming that's right, so what?"

"So what? So this! Once you know what the fight was about, you know why Di stomped Marilyn."

"Whoa, girl. Di didn't kill Marilyn."

"Marilyn fell. Do you think she'd have fallen so hard if she'd been standing steady on her pins?"

"They're coming. You didn't say any of this to me. Hear?"

"What I think," Di announced when they were settled, "is that we should not invite or give interviews on the subject of Marilyn Milledge. We should appear to be having a nice time talking among ourselves, same as always. Any wolves come sniffing around, we freeze them out fast."

Kate looked rebellious.

"You have a problem with that, Kate?"

Kate waited two beats. "Not really," she then said.

"Except I hope it doesn't mean we can't talk frankly among ourselves. Having roomed with her, I knew Marilyn rather well. I have things on my mind."

"I'm sure you do, Kate. So does Stacia, having discovered her dead body. I'm just saying, let's not have any grandstanding. Let's keep ourselves to ourselves."

"I hate two things," Kate said. "Sentimentality and hypocrisy."

"De mortuis nil nisi bonum," said Ara.

"On the other hand," said Jeremy, "whodunnit and why?"

Ara seemed ready for this. "Rumors are rife that the TC pow-wows have been explosive. Apparently Marilyn really reamed Rasene on Paper C."

"Give us a break," said Jeremy. "Rasene a killer?"

"He has an id," Kate reminded them. "So does everyone else at the Scoring. Pushed hard enough, people turn unpredictable."

They frowned over this assertion until Kate produced another reminder. "Who liked Marilyn would be a shorter list than who didn't. I didn't."

"I didn't," said Stacia.

"My major *personal* objection to the lady was based on what she'd call her scholarship," said Jeremy. "Everything else I know about her is based on Kate's gripes from last year."

"Golly," said Kate. "Does that make me an accessory?"

"Just for the record," said Di, "every drop of poison in my system shot right out the heel of my boot. Benefits of direct action."

Stacia saw Kate give Jeremy a meaningful look, which Jeremy was at pains to ignore. Did Kate not believe what Di had just said? Had she and Jeremy been whispering, hatching secret theories and suspicions?

A shiver ran through her.

"Stacia?"

It was Di who had spoken, Di whose hand was giving her arm a comforting squeeze through the soft black cashmere of her own sweater. Di who had made Marilyn vulnerable to attack, who had seen Stacia break down and cry, vulnerable too.

She shivered again.

"Guys," pleaded Di. Stacia's had a shock tonight.

"Absolutely," said Ara. "Let's go eat."

After dinner, Stacia called the hospital from the lobby pay phone, the buddies standing solemnly around. Dodge was sleeping, the nurse said. His condition was stable.

"What about concussion?" Stacia asked.

"We're monitoring for that."

"Yes, but does that mean he has a concussion?"

"Not as of this moment in time. Like I said, we're monitoring."

"Will he be discharged in the morning?"

"I couldn't tell you."

"Poor Dodge," she said when she had passed on the buddies' messages of good wishes and hung up. "All alone." *I'm* all alone, she realized she meant.

"Early bed?" suggested the ever-solicitous Di. "You've had a horrible day. Come on, I'll introduce you to Lily."

Chapter 15

The seats in Prescott Beasley's roomy old Buick were well cushioned, but Dodge, mindful of pot holes and frost heaves, was keeping himself propped on his good fist.

"It's really nice of you to pick me up, Prescott."

"Least I can do, after you risked your life."

"That's much too heroic. I was on automatic pilot."

"Point is, without you, we wouldn't have the boy. Oops. Sorry."

The Buick had hit a bad patch. My ass, Dodge thought, is in a sling. Hard to feel like a hero when your ass is in a sling.

Prescott had exaggerated: the car's plate number had delivered only Jason Armbruster's identity. According to both his mother and girlfriend, he'd taken the C.A.T.s on Saturday—math and essay. But neither woman could or would say where he was hiding himself or why he'd sought out Marilyn. Who, the medical examiner had concluded, had almost certainly been shoved. Both upper arms showed deep bruises; the base of her skull had struck the edge of the desktop with great force.

Strangest of all—Dodge couldn't get his mind around it—Jason had a record. An expert car thief who stole for fun and status, he'd agreed to steal and drive for two friends who wanted to knock off a liquor store. The friends being young and inexperienced, things got out of control.

The store owner's last act on earth had been to empty his gun into the robber who'd shot him in the stomach. The other robber escaped to Jason and the waiting car. The wounded robber survived to plea-bargain, which obliged Jason, then a few months shy of sixteen, to spend the summer in a Department of Youth Services Secure House. The brevity of the sentence rested on the plea-bargainer's inadvertent revelation that he, Jason, had not been told in advance that the plan included guns.

"A sad, sad case," Prescott now said. "Jason's father is one of those peripatetic computer engineers. He moved the family to Massachusetts when the boy was twelve. They lived in Milton for awhile, until the father decided the grass was greener someplace else. This time he went off alone. The mother's not strong. Culpably naive, I gather. To save money, she moved herself and the boy to Dorchester—to a real tough neighborhood. Luckily, someone in the junior high noticed the boy's mathematical talents and helped him get into Boston Latin.

"Now his life was divided. At school he performed well, especially in math. But he didn't seem to be able to make any friends there—Latin is exam-entrance, you know. Middle class students from the better parts of the city. Jason's friends were the young brutes in his neighborhood. DYS—the Department of Youth Services—did him some favors with that sentence. It was summer, so he didn't miss much school. And once his mother was on her own, she found her way to one of those fundamentalist fellowships. By the time the boy was paroled, the fellowship had helped her find a job and a place to live in Brookline. Where no one knew Jason's past."

"Good old America. Fresh starts for everyone."

"Yes. And don't dismiss the born again aspect."

"Is Jason born again?"

"So it appears. The car he bumped you off of belongs

to his girlfriend's father, a big shot in the fellowship. When the police arrived to make the identification, he and his daughter had just walked home from a prayer service. He was pretty surprised to learn that his car had been roving, but Jason's record sent him into shock. The daughter was shocked too, but she stood by her fella. Jason had told her he needed the car for something to do with his college applications so she gave him the keys. Believed in him, you see. Still does, she says."

"Me too. At least I'm pretty sure he didn't kill Marilyn. I went after him because he seemed as horrified and shocked as we were. Course, he could have grabbed her to threaten her, made her fall, and then been horrified and shocked by the result. But in the middle of the night, something else hit me. I had this clear impression of him holding that bakery box—by its string. I was sort of dozing, but it woke me right up. Because to grab Marilyn, he'd have to have set the box down."

"Couldn't he have picked it up again? Intending to make off with the evidence?"

"But then he'd grab it, wouldn't he? Any old which way? What I remember is too delicate and careful. The knot pinched between thumb and forefinger."

"Julia told me that Miss Steiner remembers nothing about the box. But if you're prepared to swear otherwise—"

Dodge interrupted with a discouraged grunt. "I am full of pain killers. It might have been a dream. Wish-fulfillment. Helps the kid and me too—I jumped a moving vehicle not because I'm a starry-eyed believer in youthful innocence but because of something concrete."

"Concrete?"

"His finicky grip on the cake box. Which, now I say it, isn't exactly proof positive."

Prescott slapped his steering wheel with an exasperated hand. "That dratted Ouellette woman! If she'd been paying attention, we could pinpoint how much time the boy had in there."

"I hope they find him soon. The way he tore off—part of why I went after him was that I was afraid he'd do something stupid."

"Stupid to run away."

"Yes. I just hope that's all he's done to hurt himself."

"Plenty of ways to hurt yourself when you're young and scared," agreed Prescott. "His mother says he doesn't carry much in the way of pocket money. Won't sit well with his parole officer if he steals to keep himself. Eat, I mean. By the way, doesn't it bother you that he's had trouble with the law?"

"Sure, but not in the sense that I think it shows his true colors." (*Like Othello!* cried the imp of perversity. Was it really only yesterday that he and Stacia had laughed over that? How weird, having one of the kids suddenly materialize. Word made flesh.)

Prescott sighed. "We'll know more when they find him, I suppose. Damnation! A bright boy like that—country needs all the mathematical brain power it can generate. Did you know that over half the math doctorates earned last year went to foreigners studying here? Time's coming when we'll have to import mathematicians along with computer chips and everything else."

"Wait a second, Prescott. Maybe there are some answers in his essay. Has anyone read it?"

Prescott sighed again. "Can't find it. Not easily, anyway. We've got this old batch processing system, you know. We should upgrade, but where's the money? Anyway, the people who designed our system never thought we'd need to search for an individual essay at this stage. Have to do it manually, looks like. Needle in a haystack, frankly. Cliff told the Readers this morning to watch for his name as they go."

"So you're sure it hasn't been scored already?"

"Don't even know that. By the time we got Jason's name this morning the mainframe was busy with the multiple-choice tests. Mrs. Dicenzo—you know her? In the office?—says they'll try to steal some time tonight."

The fist Dodge had been propping himself with felt on fire. Time to let the ass assume its own burdens.

"Hurts, huh? Tell you what, let's swing by the drugstore, buy you a doughnut. Used one when I had my piles done—great little invention. Probably make them out of some newfangled plastic now, but the principle's the same."

"When they find Jason, I'd like to talk to him."

"No reason you shouldn't."

"They'd let me? The police."

"Why not? You're a major witness. I'll mention it to Julia Trevor. Beautiful girl, isn't she. Woman, I should say."

"Very beautiful. How long's she been on the force?"

Beasley's laugh was knowing. "What's she doing on the force, you mean. I had a hand in that. She came to me for help when she was just a kid. Seemed to know herself pretty well. Not much of a student, more an outdoor type, wanted to work locally so she could keep her horse and so forth. How about police work, I said. After she got over being surprised she took to the idea like a duck to water. I helped her with college—the Trevors, as a clan, haven't enjoyed much worldly success—and when the old chief retired, there she was, the best qualified for the job. The selectmen pick the chief, you know. I'm proud to say I twisted some arms."

They were at the drugstore. Beasley double-parked the Buick and said he wouldn't be a minute.

Prescott, Dodge fondly thought, is what I'd like to be when I grow up. Or was having hundreds of acres of prime real estate in the family since the 1600s a prerequisite? A town like Madison reminds you what land really is—a fundament with a powerful hold on the human soul. Last night he'd assumed Julia Trevor's frosty ways were an end run around her looks and sex. Maybe, though, it was simply disdain for a landless man, someone who'd failed to set proper roots.

"Any better?"

"Much, thanks."

"No problem. As they say. Notice that? No problem means you're welcome?"

"In Winnetka what they say is yup. You say thanks, they say yup."

"I'll have to listen for that one. Winnetka. What was I just reading about Winnetka?"

"Kids there think suicide's an answer."

Prescott clucked his tongue. "You know any of them?"

"I knew one girl quite well. Not well enough, obviously. It rocked me, failing her like that. It's why I took leave."

"That's right. You told me you were on leave when I saw you the other day. I'm getting forgetful."

"Not so I notice."

Prescott waved a dismissing hand. He knew the difference between the steel trap mind he'd been born with and the bunch of junk he was saddled with now. "Here's the nut of it: If Jason is innocent, who's guilty? The woman who tromped Miss Milledge's foot the other night? What's her name again?"

"Di Royce. She's a friend of mine, so I can't think of her—well, I can't think of anyone. Course, Marilyn was pretty abrasive. She had her detractors."

"Among the Readers?"

"Yes. And we only see her once a year. Think of the people who worked with her day in and day out."

"That's right! Someone from the outside!"

The old man's sudden burst of optimism was painful to witness. He slapped the steering wheel and went on. "I want this whole business cleared up as close to now as humanly possible. And with minimum publicity. I've agreed to a press conference later this morning—our lawyer says they'll go for the jugular if we don't cooperate. I must say I'm dreading it. Ever notice how anti-intellectual media people are? Television people especially? It's the *authority* of the intellect they hate—rivals their own authority, you see. Anyway, I want the C.A.T.s exonerated. Maybe you can help."

"Be glad to," said Dodge with much more conviction than he felt. Undeniably, the C.A.T.s provided his old friend and supporter with a life's work, an ongoing cause. They were also an occasion of severe stress to an extremely vulnerable population. No one, he firmly believed, was as vulnerable as a seventeen-year-old. The securities of childhood riddled with doubts, the rewards of adulthood impossibly beyond reach. And probably a con anyway.

Last night, Jason's anguished face had kept eliding into Courtney's. *My parents don't care, Mr. Hackett. No one cares. I could totally disappear from the face of the earth and they'd never notice. Then they'll be like, oh, hey, let's call Magnum, P.I., let's put her face on the milk cartons. Except it'll be too late.*

They swung into the drive leading to the Center. The Green World, Dodge suddenly realized. Right up there with the Forest of Arden and Prospero's Island. A realm of enchantment, where even the police chief is beautiful. He hoped his belief in Jason's innocence wasn't just fairy dust in his eyes. "Must be nice," he observed to Prescott, "to call all this your own."

"It's nice but it's a responsibility. I'm grateful to the Trust for sharing the essential stewardship."

"I'm grateful too. It's great, working here in peace and quiet. Getting to breathe so much good air."

"The Scorings are fun, aren't they? Community of colleagues, lively conversations wherever you turn?"

Supplication. Murder had blown a hole in Prescott's dream; he needed reassurance. Dodge took a second to imagine Stacia lithe on the exercise mat. "In many ways," he then said, "they're the most fun an English teacher ever gets."

Prescott braked under the porte-cochere. "I better warn you. There's some panic afoot. Four Readers took off early this morning. Cliff's laid on round-the-clock security guards, but they weren't persuaded. Three women and a man. And can you beat it? Man's room wasn't even on the first floor!"

"Four's no exodus."

"There may be more by now. I wish they'd find the boy."

Dodge blinked in surprise. "I really doubt he's a killer, Prescott."

"I still wish they'd find him."

Dodge said goodbye, thanks again, and achieved a gingerly exit.

Walking hurt less than sitting.

Cheered by this finding, he made an effort to appreciate the old man's point of view. If Jason had killed Marilyn, and Jason were found, the crisis was over, the C.A.T.s were safe. If not, not.

All right. Forgive Prescott who hadn't seen Jason frozen with fear and horror. Or watched in relentless and accusatory slow motion, his features dissolving into Courtney's.

Courtney could no longer be saved, but there was hope for Jason. And because Dodge did not intend to make the same mistake twice there was also hope for him.

"Mr. Hackett?"

The young woman who stepped from behind Jason's yew bushes to intercept Dodge had a nose red from the cold and a winning smile. She handed him her card. "Jill Brower, *North Shore News*. I've been waiting here in the hope that you can tell me something about Jason Armbruster."

"He said he didn't do it and I believed him. That's really all I know, but please print it. Jason might see it and turn himself in."

"What about the fight between Di Royce and Marilyn Milledge?"

"What fight?"

"Come on, Mr. Hackett. I've been talking to your colleagues. Everyone says you know exactly what Ms. Royce was angry about."

The buddies, clearly, were hanging tough, keeping their mouths shut for Di's sake. Just as clearly, Jill Brower was trespassing. As soon as he had to, Dodge could say "no comment" and duck inside where she'd be afraid to follow. "I saw what everyone saw. Marilyn fell. Twisted her ankle, I guess. What's that got to do with Jason?"

The smile grew more winning. "Apparently Ms. Royce has an alibi for the time of death. Should the police believe her?"

"Of course."

"Say you had some idea what the two women were fighting about. If I knew what you knew, it would be easier for me to focus on Jason. Then, as you yourself said, he might see my story and—"

"What I myself said was that I saw no fight. Period. I've got to go now. Will you be at the press conference? Fine. I'll call Prescott Beasley—that was him dropping me off."

"I know. His Buick's famous all over the North Shore. What are you going to call him about?"

"Your special interest in Di Royce."

She didn't like this. "There's no need Mr. Hackett. Thanks all the same."

"No trouble. Glad to help."

"Then please don't say anything. This is my own angle I don't want the other reporters moving in on it."

"I don't understand."

"This is the working press, not Woodward and Bernstein. To them the story is Jason, with maybe a sidebar on the C.A.T.s. They'll get their copy, meet their deadlines and go home. Same as I'd do if I hadn't heard Marilyn Milledge talk one night. Ever since then I've suspected she's one, full of shit and two, ripping off the feminist movement. So, for my own curiosity, I'm donating overtime."

An unexpected twist, almost tempting. But Dodge's primary loyalty was to Di. "All right. I won't contact Prescott."

She thanked him and he opened the door to go in. "If you change your mind on the fight," she called after him, "you've got my number."

Chapter 16

Doughnut ringing his good arm, Dodge found the Readers near the close of a break period.

"Good to have you back, Dodger."

"Thanks," he said to a man he'd never seen before in his life. As if this were a signal, he was suddenly surrounded by other strangers and near-strangers, Readers who wanted to hear from his own lips what had happened last night.

Cliff Rasene, at the podium, was calling for the resumption of the Scoring. The doughnut his battering ram, Dodge made his way to Table Fifteen.

Stacia, funereal in Di's black sweater and skirt, let out a little yelp at the sight of his splinted and bandaged hand. "'It's just to immobilize it," Dodge explained "Rest the tendons. Nothing's broken. I'm fine."

Instead of answering, she put her arms around him and gave him a close, gentle hug. He could feel her breath against his neck. Her hair smelled like lemon. He yearned to nuzzle her adorable nape, but didn't dare.

Rasene begged the noisy room to settle down and get back to work.

"Man's a spoilsport," said Dodge. "Pay him no heed."

But Stacia released him. (All good students, which is to say, all teachers, hesitate to get on the wrong side of authority.) "Are you really all right?"

"Yes. What about you?"

"I'm fine."

TC Francie came up. "Can you bubble your own paper, Dodge?"

"To bubble" was the C.A.T. verb for filling in the tiny circles that told the computer who you were and how you'd scored the essay. Dodge assured her he was sufficiently ambidextrous to bubble lefty.

"Let's start, then. Cliff's about to have a bird."

Dodge settled himself on his doughnut. But where was Will Blodgett, the newcomer who belonged on Ellie Ostergard's left?

"Jumped ship," Ellie whispered. "Didn't even wait for breakfast. And you know what's worse? His room wasn't even on the first floor. I had a paper this morning with a wonderful phrase: spineless amoeba. Sums up young Will, don't you think?"

Francie shushed them.

Dodge opened his folder. *I disagree with the quote. Chain gangs have been totally replaced by the revolving door policy. A furlowed murderer raped and killed again first chance he got. Is this justice?*

The ballroom had grown quiet—a thick, oppressive quiet. No giggles, no whispers.

Dodge scrawled Stacia a note: *Why's everyone being so good?*

Fear, she wrote back.

It was lunchtime. "Before we break," Rasene announced, "I want to honor the promise I made this morning to keep you informed of news as we receive it. Unfortunately, there's little to report. Jason Armbruster is still missing. We still have no idea why he came to the Center or sought out Marilyn. Again, if any of you can shed light on any of this, do call Chief Trevor at any time.

"Stress is making our Cliff repetitious," murmured Mark Agresti.

"I have been assured that the investigation is proceeding on all fronts. The Massachusetts State Police and their cohorts in Pennsylvania, where Marilyn taught, are working closely with Chief Trevor. In the meantime, please know that the Center staff, the Master Readers, and myself are fully aware of the strain this sad event has put you under. As I said this morning, anyone wishing to go home is quite free to do so. I hope you will understand that I hope you don't find it necessary to leave. I hope you will take comfort from the presence of our skilled and capable security patrol."

"I hope you'll stop saying hope," said Agresti.

"Tomorrow, Saturday," Rasene went on, "at the close of the work day, there will be a short memorial service in the lounge."

An image of Marilyn, her voice caressing Cole Porter, flooded Dodge's memory.

"If I can hold you another minute," Rasene said, "I'd like to share a note I received this morning from a Reader. *I know,* she writes, *that I'm not the only one who is frightened. I also know that Marilyn would challenge us, as she so often did in her scholarly work, to rise above our fears. It therefore seems to me, and to others with whom I have spoken, that to complete this Scoring in a calm and professional manner would be a fitting tribute to the intellectual courage and daring of a truly remarkable colleague.*"

Rasene laid the page tenderly down. Clapping, scattered, then vigorous, filled the room. Joe Callahan, possibly prompted by Cole Porter, led the applause at Table Fifteen.

"Puke," Stacia muttered with each clap, "puke, puke, puke."

Agresti heard her and snickered. "Think it's a plant?" he asked.

This division, hagiologists on one side, skeptics on the other, became general by midafternoon. Shadowing, darkening, this division was a related one: Most Readers believed that Marilyn had been a deliberately selected target of violence. A vocal and growing minority, however, insisted that she'd been killed at random. Which meant that any one of them might be next on Jason's list.

Jason! Only the most ivory-tower readers were immune to the name's horrific associations—maniacal blood lust, a hockey mask hiding God knows what, screams in the night.

But, of course Dodge and Stacia might be right and the kid innocent. In that case—it had to be faced—the killer might very well be one of them.

Chapter 17

When Dodge returned to his room that night, his roommate was suiting up for a powerwalk. "Howdy, Pardner," Frank said.

As a flea joins a dog, Frank had joined Dodge and Stacia for lunch. A woman at their table had observed that the roommates were partners in crime- (pause, arch smile) *prevention*. By now, everyone seemed to have heard that Frank had played a significant role in last night's chase.

"Howdy, Frank. Going out?"

"Don't worry. We're a group."

Frank looked pleased with himself. He was in a group. Popular.

"Oh," he went on. "This was under the door."

He handed Dodge a sealed envelope. The message inside was from Prescott Beasley, asking Dodge to phone or stop by before dinner. Prescott would be happy to pick him up.

Dodge's injuries preventing Nautilus, he could use the short walk to Prescott's cottage. Did Rasene's warning against being outdoors alone after dark apply to him? He decided it didn't.

Frank was waiting expectantly, hoping to be briefed on Dodge's message. Dodge decided to ignore him along with the warning.

Prescott, looking tired, was an uncharacteristically fussed host. Dodge and his doughnut had to try three different chairs. When he picked one of the chintz-covered pair near the fireplace, Prescott insisted on lighting the logs laid earlier by Doris. Laid imperfectly; more fussing. Dodge wasn't allowed to help. Nor could he help with the drinks.

Out in the kitchen, a tray of ice cubes fell from Prescott's hands and spilled noisily. Butter stopped bashing at Dodge's thigh and pattered off to investigate.

At length, the two men were settled, drinks in hand, Butter at his master's side.

"How was the press conference?" Dodge asked.

"Long and self-important."

"Was anyone interested in why Marilyn was using a cane?"

Prescott, whose hearing was superb, cupped a hand behind his ear. Dodge repeated his question. "Oh, that. I'm not even sure it came up. Maybe once, in passing. Mostly they concentrated on Scoring procedures—the way this place works, how much security we've got, whether the Readers' names are circulated in advance. But I wanted to talk to you about something else. In confidence.''

"Of course,'' said Dodge.

"The police have a solid clue. Not for publication. I got it from Julia, of course. Wednesday evening, between five and five-thirty, a car was stolen from the parking lot of the Stop & Shop where Jason works. Woman came out of the store with her shopping bags and found an empty space. By Thursday morning, the car was back. Unharmed, no fingerprints. But it just so happens that before this woman did her grocery shopping, she'd picked that car up at a gas station right nearby. Oil change and lubrication. The exact mileage figure written right on the slip. The odometer reading Thursday morning was that figure plus what could be one round trip from the Stop & Shop to Madison.''

"So Jason could have been here Wednesday night.''

"Exactly.''

"He could have been outside the lounge, watching and listening, when Di Royce stomped Marilyn. We were all talking about it afterwards—he could have heard any one of us saying Marilyn's name.''

"And then, the next night, asked for her at the desk.''

Dodge nodded. "Why, though? What did he want from her?''

Prescott's encouraging smile faded. Clearly he'd expected an answer from Dodge instead of more questions.

"Maybe,'' Dodge began, "it has something to do with Marilyn being famous enough for *People* magazine. Born-agains like their women traditional, don't they? Here's Marilyn with all these sex-role challenges—maybe she comes across as Satan's handmaid. Except then you have to wonder how a kid in Brookline knows that this evil creature is scheduled for the Scoring."

"Could he have read a newspaper story? An interview?"

"It's possible. My students are always bringing me articles about the C.A.T.s—although it's usually the parents who spot them. Maybe Mrs. Armbruster read something and mentioned it to Jason. The police could ask."

Prescott reached for his notepad and jotted himself a reminder. "There's something else," he then said. "I've just been notified that the mainframe has finished with the math tests. Guess what our boy scored?"

"Not an 800."

"Bullseye."

"Jesus. Smart kid. Still. He could've blown the essay. Sometimes they freeze, can't produce a line. He could've come up here, looking for someone to blame. He sees Di Royce go after Marilyn and gets a great idea. No, forget it. Makes no sense."

"Keep chewing away, will you? And let's meet again tomorrow evening. This whole business—I have to have someone to talk to. Julia's doing her job, but Julia's got her limits. I think I mentioned that she wasn't ever much of a student. Doesn't know her way round the academy. I have to footnote everything for her. Wears me out. So if you can spare the time—"

"I'll be glad to do what I can, Prescott. The stolen car's a bad break. Just what the police need to settle in with the idea of Jason as main suspect."

"If the boy is innocent, he should come forth, Julia keeps saying."

"Yeah, well. Could be he doesn't trust the blindness of justice. His stint at the DYS might have taught him some contrary truths. But I'm wearing you out myself, Prescott. Why don't I let you get to your supper?"

"Care to join me? On second thought, I'd best give you a rain check. You're right. I am tired—too tired for company. But you see why I want this kept quiet, don't you? The possibility that the boy was spying around the Center is damned nasty. Nerve-wracking. Cliff Rasene tells me no one else has asked to leave, and I want to keep it that way."

"I'm a tomb," Dodge assured him.

"I know you are. I'm one too. If this blows up in my face, you never heard anything I said tonight."

"I don't follow."

"Our lawyer's jittery. He says the only course reliably free of tort action from the Readers is prompt and full disclosure of any and all information that might bear on their safety. Nuts to that, I told him. A whole generation of college-bound kids is counting on every single Reader to sit tight until the job's done. That's the Beasley Center's mission, and no nervous nellie of a lawyer's going to wreck it."

Dodge was back at the Center in time to have a pre-dinner drink with the buddies. But he felt distracted, out of it, unable to fathom how his friends could invest such passion and care on the revision of their sleeping arrangements.

Finally it was settled. Di would move down to the room Stacia and Marilyn had shared, with, naturally, Ara for protection. Stacia would sleep in third-floor safety with Di's designated roommate Lily Freese.

Di had done well by doing good. Ara was happy and so, presumably, was Stacia. She certainly looked happy and had some color back in her face helped by her red sweater. It was the bulky one he'd first seen her in, coming into the ballroom late and flustered.

Stacia's name tag was still pinned dead center, her chest still looked flat. But hadn't she felt soft, womanly, when she'd hugged him this morning? Or was that only his imagination and need?

"Dodge!" Kate cried. "You haven't heard the great news! Congratulate Jeremy Cheatham, the C.A.T.s newest and baddest Table Captain."

Jeremy grinned. "It's true. I have benefitted from the misfortune of another."

"We feel," Kate intoned, imitating Rasene, "that Jeremy's promotion is a truly fitting tribute to a truly remarkable colleague."

Jeremy held up a cautionary hand. "Some will point out that the misfortune I have benefitted from is my own."

Being born black, Dodge knew he meant, and thus, in the rarified environment of the Center, first in line among the Readers experienced enough to fill in for Marilyn. His reference to his own misfortune was knee-jerk Blackspeak. Knee-jerk Whitespeak was the only possible response. Dodge didn't feel up to inventing any.

"Oh pooh," said Kate. "Everyone knows you're a QN, Jeremy."

Jeremy's laugh was quick and surprised.

"QN?" asked Ara.

"Quality nigger," Kate explained. "As opposed to TN, token nigger."

"I haven't heard that one since Great Society days," said Jeremy.

"Rob still uses it,' said Kate. "My husband. He's the last surviving Great Society liberal. No mean feat for an upper-income black tarheel. Course he *does* work for a tobacco company. Gives him lots of practice handling contradictions."

Astonishment had lifted Di's eyebrows out of sight behind her bangs. "What black tarheel? Who's black?"

"Rob. Didn't you know? I thought I'd mentioned it."

As the talk moved interestingly into interracial and other

kinds of mixed marriages, Dodge, as surprised as the rest by Kate's revelation, relaxed on his doughnut. For a minute there, against the grim backdrop of Jason's plight, the buddies had seemed a little frivolous. Shallow.

Stacia said something that Dodge, preoccupied, didn't catch. Everyone else laughed. What a difference a day makes, he thought. She's in. I'm somewhere else. On another planet.

Chapter 18

By Saturday, most of the Richmond Street Pentacostal Fellowship knew that one of their lambs had strayed and was feared lost. Among the members, an influential minority argued that Jason Armbruster was no lamb but a wolf in sheep's clothing. A wolf, they insisted, made infinitely more dangerous by his disappearance. Among the outraged was the sexton, Mr. Mackie. "That pretty boy?" Mr. Mackie inquired of his wife. "The one you're so sweet on? Turns out he's a killer. A ruthless killer, with a police record long as all eternity."

A satisfied expression on his face, Mr. Mackie went off to work. The fellowship owned a real church, formerly Presbyterian, its purchase enabled by a complex confluence of preservationist activism and population shifts. Mr. Mackie took pride in the handsome brownstone structure. It was his conscientious pleasure, every Saturday morning, to perform a pre-Sabbath inspection.

This particular morning, spray cleaner in one hand, sponge in the other, he noticed damp spots on the washroom's roller towel. The last time anyone had been authorized to use the premises—Mr. Mackie loved the solemn weight of this phrase—was Thursday night, for choir practice.

Neighborhood kids? But kids left different kinds of evidence. Beer cans and piles of burnt matches.

Sanctuary. Straight from a forgotten childhood matinee, the word barreled into Mr. Mackie's awareness: hunchbacked Charles Laughton, horrible and desperate, scrambling up the church tower. *Sanctuary! Sanctuary!*

Heart crazy in his chest, Mr. Mackie fled to the safety of a crowded drugstore. There he found a pay phone and called the police.

Shortly after the squad cars had surrounded the church, Jason was found in a basement closet, hidden among the Nativity costumes. One officer told him his rights while another cuffed his hands behind his back. In due course he was bundled northward, to the Essex County Jail.

Jan Dicenzo handed Rasene the news on a slip of paper twenty minute before the end of that day's session.

Rasene's elation was immediately tempered by practicality. Should he wait out the clock? Certainly little work would get done in the jubilant aftermath. And they were so far behind! Mop-up—the reconvening after Christmas of Readers who lived within driving distance—was going to last an expensive forever.

On the other hand any number of Readers must have looked up from their work to observe Mrs. Dicenzo's entrance and the passage of the liberating news. It would run through the Scoring like wildfire—the heartless slave driver had let them suffer for twenty extra minutes! On top of what they'd already endured!

Fearing their wrath, he cleared his throat and approached the mike.

Tall and handsome in her polished boots and belted, full-skirted, gray suit, Julia Trevor waited for Dodge to come out of the ballroom. Rather than brooding on why she was here—she owed Prescott too much to cross him—she mentally reviewed her session with Jason Armbruster and Brendan Connolly, the detective the state had assigned to the case.

Connolly was ready to call it an open and shut case. He had taken pains to remind her of the huge quantity of unsolved murders on the Commonwealth's books. "Unsolved due to the simple fact of no confessions or eyewitnesses. Which, no matter what they put on the TV or tell the taxpayer, is how killers get brought to trial around here. This time, what do we have? A kid caught red-handed by two terrific eyewitnesses. Teachers, Julia. Pillars of the community."

"They think he's innocent," Julia said, not for the first time.

"They're civilians, that's their prerogative. I'm talking *case*. What's your problem? You like the laddie's looks?"

In fact, Julia didn't like Jason at all. Under his politeness she saw arrogance—the conceit of someone who thinks he's smarter than everyone else. Who thinks he's too good to tell a couple of cops what he was doing at the Center and why he'd run away from what had to be at least manslaughter.

Connolly, miles ahead of himself, wanted to go for murder one, and thus nail down the lesser charge of manslaughter. The kid, he reminded Julia, had deliberately sought out the deceased, implying malice. He'd premeditated to the extent of boosting that car from the supermarket lot.

"Yes, that was me," Jason had admitted to them with calm matter-of-factness. "I needed it."

"You always take what you need?" Julia asked.

"Of course not! That would be against the Eighth Commandment. But this time the Lord gave me no choice."

"Uh-huh. What about your parole conferences with Mrs. Rosenberg?"

"Wednesday I was busy. Friday I was hiding."

"Gee, Jason," Connolly drawled, "would of been nice if you'd given the lady a ring. Courtesy counts."

Jason's composure was not dented by the detective's sarcasm. "I know. I was just too busy. I've prayed that Mrs. Rosenberg will forgive me."

"Mrs. Rosenberg's forgiveness isn't gonna bat you in, Champ," said Connolly. "Do you understand the phrase 'released to the community on condition of liberty'?"

"Yes."

"Explain it to me."

"I'm free on the condition that I stay out of trouble and meet with Mrs. Rosenberg every Wednesday and Friday until my eighteenth birthday."

"Very good, Jason. So how's it look to you? Aren't you kinda up shit creek?"

Jason had closed his eyes. His lips moved in soundless speech. This, Connolly and Julia had decided, was praying. It was how the kid had met every reference to the legal machinery that was poised to overwhelm him.

Julia gave it another try. "Monday, when court's in session again after the weekend, you'll have your hearing. I hope by then you're ready to explain what you were doing in Marilyn Milledge's room."

Jason kept praying.

She had one more thing to say to the closed, remote face. "The man you just about crippled Friday night? Dodge Hackett? He'll be coming around to see you."

After a second, the lips stopped moving. Opening his eyes, Jason smiled, thanked her, and said he'd been praying for this very thing.

"Why's that?" Connolly asked.

"I want to tell him—Mr. Hackett, right?—how sorry I am for hurting him."

The Readers, emerging from the ballroom, chattered in excited relief. The Killer Teen had been caught; they were safe again. Only Dodge and Stacia looked worried, thoughtful.

Julia approached them and told Dodge she wanted a word with him.

"Shouldn't Stacia come too?" Dodge asked. "She was as much a witness as—"

"No. Just you."

Alone with Dodge in Jan Dicenzo's office, Julia speedily summarized what she and Connolly had learned from Jason. She then made it clear that she was involving Dodge only under duress. "Prescott's pushed me out on a limb. I accept that, but I won't accept you pushing me off. You'll report to me, and you'll report everything. No more hero stuff with moving vehicles. No secret agendas. You or Prescott get some bright idea, you run it by me before you make the slightest move."

"Sounds fine. You're the pro. I'm just trying to make Prescott's life easier."

"Really. I got the impression that your major interest was the boy."

"Nope. Prescott comes first. Course, I do harbor a firm belief in the presumption of innocence."

"I'll ignore that, Mr. Hackett. Jason's anxious to talk to you. Prescott says you can borrow his car. You know the way to the courthouse? Good." She handed him her card. "They'll give you fifteen minutes with him. That's you, Mr. Hackett, not you and Ms. Steiner. And you'll call me the minute you're done."

"Got it." Dodge, rising, tried hard not to sound too dry.

But the chief wasn't finished with him. "Prescott asked me to tell you that a Teddy Massack will be representing Jason."

Another old school tie, one of Boston's best known trial lawyers. Prescott must be footing the bill. "Good man, Teddy."

"So I understand. One other thing—they finally found Jason's essay. You'll have to read it here—C.A.T. rules say it can't go out of this room. Also, I hope you know better than to discuss its contents with the media."

She handed him the closely written page. Not since *Fanny Hill*, encountered at fifteen, had the written word stirred in Dodge so much strange commotion.

Jason had printed, pressing hard, the embossed effect threatening legibility. *Humans,* Dodge deciphered, *are born in sin, which is the total opposite of freedom. Then they dedicate their lives to forging new chains of sin.*

The teacher in Dodge registered redundancy. Also, he disliked "human" as a noun, and "total" always irritated. Still, as writing, it wasn't bad. A three, if the kid stayed on this level, a four if he improved as he warmed to his subject.

Then a thought blasted these pedagogic meanderings to smithereens. He turned the page over. Two Readers' codes were properly entered and bubbled.

"Who are they?" he asked.

"Marilyn Milledge and Frances Squires. Ms. Milledge scored it a three, Ms. Squires a four. Whatever that tells us."

It told Dodge a chilling plenty. Jason's essay, plucked from the mass by the pollster's science had been read early by the Table Captains, before any of the Readers arrived.

It now seemed unarguable that design, not chance, had drawn the kid to Marilyn's room. Marilyn, in grotesque violation of C.A.T. codes of confidentiality and trust, must have contacted him.

Jason's phone number was right on his paper's heading, along with his name and address. Had Marilyn called him up? Chastised him for redundancy and the use of "human" as a noun? Encouraged him to think that if they could meet in person she might change his score? But then why the elaborate charade with the cake and false identity? Why steal a car to check things out?

"Does Jason," he asked the chief, "know you're aware that Marilyn scored his essay?"

"Of course."

"What was his reaction?"

Julia produced a puckery smile. "Cornered, Jason communicates only with God."

"Poor Prescott. The media's going to kill him. Thousands of helpless students laid bare to the slings and arrows of outrageous academics."

"He hasn't been told yet. If you're ready, I'll drive you over so you can pick up his car."

"Want me to break the bad news to him?"

"I've known Prescott my whole life, Mr. Hackett. I'm quite capable of handling bad news on my own."

Chapter 19

Dodge had worked, the summer he was twenty, as an aide in a state mental hospital. The squalor and despair of that place came back to him in the interview room of the county jail. The smell was identical—food long boiled, ripe bodies, pine disinfectant splashed around to mask without cleaning.

A mesh divider and tables, bolted to the floor, divided the room and its scarred wooden armchairs. Dodge sat on one, glad of his doughnut. A loutish guard brought Jason in and gave him a push in the direction of the chair opposite.

Dodge hardly recognized the kid. The way his hair was matted over one ear gave him a lopsided look. His lips were tensely puckered, bleached of normal color. Long dark lashes emphasized the shadows under his eyes. A cluster of bright pimples grew in his chin stubble.

Dodge introduced himself and said he was a Reader at the C.A.T. Scoring.

"I know who you are, Mr. Hackett. I'm sorry I hurt you. I've prayed and prayed you'll forgive me."

Now that the kid had roused himself—he sounded genuinely contrite—Dodge was better able to understand why Mrs. Ouellette had called him a living doll. "I went after you because I believed you were innocent and I wanted to stop you long enough to tell you that. Once my ass stops hurting I'll forget all about it. You learn that trick watching car chases on TV?''

"I guess."

"TV's got a lot to answer for, doesn't it? As you pointed out in your essay, it chains us with cravings for flashy consumer goods.''

Jason took this in wary silence, as if suspecting a trick.

"I read your essay just this afternoon," Dodge continued. "You did a good job. Good sentence structure, good mechanical control. On that basis alone, I'd have given it a three, which is what it got from Ms. Milledge.''

At "Milledge," Jason squeezed his eyes shut. Alerted by Chief Trevor, Dodge assumed this was praying. He pressed breezily ahead. "I give extra credit for qualities like passion and conviction. I like to find a real sense of life on the page. So if your essay had come my way, I'd have given it a four. Same as Ms. Squires did.''

The boy's eyes flew open. The hopefulness that suddenly lit his face nearly broke Dodge's heart. And, come to think, probably exonerated Francie from any involvement in this mess.

"You're obviously bright, Jason. Obviously you'll do well in whatever college is lucky enough to have you as a student. Your essay indicates that you care about this country and where it's heading. I'm sure you know how much America needs the energy and talent of her brightest young citizens. So. You said you wanted me to forgive you.''

"I've prayed and prayed you would."

Tit for tat was what Dodge had been trying to set up. The kid's response, making God the deal's middleman, was a curve ball. Intentional? Impossible to say. But best play it soft and warm, not cagey. "I do forgive you, Jason. I forgive you and I care what happens to you. I want to help you move all this trouble behind you. So does Dr. Beasley, and the rest of the people at the Center. We want to help you work things out so you can get on with your life. Pretty clearly, Ms. Milledge contacted you. What did she say?''

Jason flinched back into prayer.

"You're a Christian, you can't lie to me. But I notice you're not denying she contacted you. It was absolutely wrong of her to do that. No teacher at the Scoring is supposed to do anything like that, ever. She upset you, and no wonder. Tell me the rest. Let the blame fall where it belongs—on the instigator.''

Jason's lips moved faster.

"Time's up," the guard announced in a bored voice.

"Just a second, officer. Think, Jason. Think of your future! Talk now and it's a short item on the back pages of a couple of newspapers. Keep up the mystery man routine and they'll put you on national TV. Is that going to impress anyone in college admissions?''

The guard approached and gave Jason's arm a rough yank.

Inspired by the kid's perfectly normal glare of anger, Dodge lobbed in a parting shot. "Remember, Jason—God helps those who help themselves.''

The boy wrenched loose. Fury skinned his cheeks taut and showed every tooth in his mouth. "Get out of here! Get out! The Lord will not be mocked! I never want to see you again!''

Smirking as if gratified, the guard hustled his prisoner from the room.

Dodge put the Buick in Prescott's garage and walked around to the front door. Still raw after Jason's outburst, he had little left for Prescott, sure to be deeply troubled by Marilyn's apparent breach. Still, the car keys had to be returned.

A figure appeared on the shadowed walk between driveway and cottage. A needle of fear ran through Dodge. *Readers should not walk about alone after dark*. But it was only Tank Beasley, explaining in rushed, low tones that he'd come to "do about Gramper."

"What about the kid?" Tank then demanded. "He say anything new?"

"No."

"Thank God." Tank's heartfelt exhalation matched anything Jason had produced. Was the whole world going religioso? "Gramper's got plenty on his plate as it is. He wants to see you, but keep it quick and simple, okay? I'm really worried about him. This place is his life, and it's tough when your ivory tower turns out to have clay feet."

In a sudden illumination, Dodge knew exactly what kind of C.A.T. essay Tank had written, back in his own schooldays. But that wasn't fair. He knew Tank only by sight—probably because anyone originally encountered as a grimy little lower-former tended to remain beneath notice forever. On the positive side, Tank cared enough about Prescott to be here, offering his support in a dark hour. Also, he had grown tall and polished. Nothing grimy about his longish, well cut hair, his tweed jacket and sharply creased flannels.

Prescott didn't rise from his chair. The hand he held out to Dodge was cold and shaky. Butter, too, seemed enfeebled. Instead of his usual aggressive welcome, he stayed on the hearth rug, giving it a few halfhearted slaps of his tail.

"Tank's built a nice fire and we're having a little snort. What's yours? No, no, Tank will get it. You sit down—got your gadget? Good. Tell me about the boy."

Keep it quick and simple, Tank had said. Dodge saw no reason to burden the old man with Jason's blow-up or his own stupidity in causing it. "Not much to tell, I'm afraid. He's sorry he hurt me and wanted me to forgive him. I tried to make that a condition of him leveling with me about what happened, but no dice.''

"He strike you as a real believer?''

"Oh yes. He uses prayer to hide, but so did Joan of Arc.''

"You'll try again tomorrow?''

"If you want me to, sure. Thanks, Tank.''

The beer Tank had handed him tasted good. Talking to Jason had been thirsty work.

"We've got a new development,'' Prescott said. "Right after you left, a call came into the office from Texas. Small-town lady, simple soul. She'd caught a news report about Miss Milledge on CNN and remembered that her son, who'd just taken the C.A.T.s, had received a postcard from someone of the same name.''

"A postcard.''

"Her son had thrown it away, unfortunately. She remembered that Miss Milledge had taken him to task for devoting so much time to athletics and his four-by-four. Tank has explained to me that a four-by-four is a species of automobile.''

"Was she upset?''

"Excited, Mrs. Dicenzo said. Thrilled to have a connection with someone mentioned on TV.''

"Jason must've gotten a postcard too.''

"Julia's looking for it. And Mrs. Dicenzo's started a search for the rest of the essays Miss Milledge scored— something we should have done right away. God knows how long it's going to take, or how many more postcards she sent. Our lawyer is howling his head off. I howled some myself. What in Sam Hill possessed the woman?''

"I'm as sorry as I can be, Prescott. It's terrible.''

Tank, who'd pulled up a chair between them, gave his thighs a brisk slap. "Dodge is too polite to tell you, Gramper, but he's already late for an evening date.''

"Of course he is. Sorry to've kept you, Dodge."

"I'll see you tomorrow," Dodge said, standing. "Okay if I borrow the Buick again? Great car. Drives like a dream."

Tank was on his feet too. "You sprung for a top lawyer, Gramper, shouldn't you buy Dodge a rental? Since he's doing all this running around for you?"

"Good idea," said Prescott.

"I'll call Jimmy Monahan, set it up for you, Dodge. Jimmy's local—he'll deliver the car right to the Center."

"Tank?" Prescott quavered. "Are you leaving too?"

"Just giving Dodge a lift back, Gramper. Won't be a minute."

"I can walk, Tank."

"Not on my watch you can't."

It was a three-minute drive. Tank had just enough time to bewail his grandfather's weakened condition—"Pathetic, isn't it? You hear how he asked if I was leaving?"—and thank Dodge for helping ease the old man's mind.

Dodge found his friends in the lounge, finishing their last round before dinner.

"Mr. Donut!" cried Kate.

"What news from the slammer?" asked Ara.

The last thing Dodge wanted to discuss. Before he could answer, Di cut in. " 'The clink,' folks around Mohawk say."

For the next few minutes, the air was thick with other candidates—the pokey, jailhouse, big house, the Rock, in stir, in the jug, the hoosegow, can, lockup, brig, pen.

Only Stacia continued to look as if she hoped to hear something serious about Jason. Through the grace of word play, laughter and his gulped double bourbon, Dodge found it possible to avoid her concerned eye. Maybe later, if the two of them were alone together, he'd

110

explain that he'd gotten nothing out of the kid and blown it to boot.

Alone with Stacia, he could fix it so she wouldn't criticize him. Loyal support from the buddies was by no means as predictable. Which was a fairly appalling insight. So far, Prescott's attempt to turn him into a detective had revealed too little on the murder, too much on his own flawed self.

Chapter 20

Midway through dinner, Dodge saw Mrs. Ouellette enter and scan the dining hall. Spotting Cliff Rasene, she went to his table and handed him a note. Rasene, who must have noted the buddies' noisy, tardy arrival, came right over.

Di's back was to him, so she didn't notice his approach until the note was under her nose. "For you," Rasene said, and beat a fast retreat.

"Extraordinary man," Di informed her friends. "Uh-oh. Chief Trevor wants a word with me. Another word, she lacks the manners to say."

Di, of course, had already been questioned the night of the murder. More lengthily than any of them, including Ara, her alibi. But then Ara hadn't stomped Marilyn.

"Finish your dinner first," Ara said.

"Right," said Di. "The condemned woman ate a hearty meal."

Brave as this sounded, before long she dropped her knife and fork with a clatter. She jumped to her feet and was gone, Ara's quick hands catching her chair before it crashed over backward.

To wait for Di, the rest of them moved to the lounge, where they found their usual corner occupied by Frank St. Leger and two other Readers. By the time the buddies had collected their drinks, only Frank remained.

Ara, who refused on principle to wear a watch, had to ask again what time it was.

"Di's been gone approximately twenty minutes," Kate said. "Relax. Maybe the beauteous chief is checking out Di's feminist credentials."

"Why would she do that?"

"A small town policeperson has to be one of the boys, right? Otherwise she'd never survive. So what's feminism to her? Something weird and extreme. Confrontive. For all she knows, Di and Marilyn tangled over some ideological difference."

Ara grew fearsomely alert. "Kate? Did you happen to wonder along those lines in the hearing of the police?"

"Me? I'm the three wise monkeys."

"Fuzz don't be liking monkey business," said Jeremy, who had found his own interview reminiscent of various boyhood traumas. "They be calling it obstruction of justice."

"Tough," said Kate.

"Here's Di now," Frank said in a low voice.

"No need to *warn* us," Kate told him, loftily disregarding historic truth. "We don't say things behind each other's backs that we wouldn't say face to face."

Di was in terrible shape. As he had the first night, Ara sprang into action, getting her seated next to him and drinking from his glass.

The ice cubes shifted, splashing her. She gave her nose

and mouth an impatient wipe with the back of her hand. "All right, let's have it," she then said in a rough voice. "Who blabbed?"

"Blabbed what?" asked Kate.

"What you saw in the elevator Wednesday evening. What I made crystal clear to you was my business and mine alone."

No one said a word.

"Look, it's done. At least give me this one courtesy. Dodge? Jeremy? Kate?"

"Not me," said Jeremy.

Dodge and Kate shook their heads. Kate crossed her heart.

But Di was looking at Frank. "Why is that man about to shit a brick?"

It's Frank's dream come true, Dodge thought. He's the cynosure of every buddy's eye.

"Talk, Frank," advised Ara.

"No one told me it was a secret. I didn't know!"

"Yeah," said Di, loading the word with megatons of cruel disregard. "What did you actually say?"

"Chief Trevor introduced herself and I said, right, I've seen you before. She wanted to know where, and I said getting into a car with Di Royce, Wednesday night. That wasn't me, she said, and asked if I'd seen any strangers around the Center since."

"And then?"

"That's all. I was doing my powerwalk—"

"Fuck your powerwalk. You got the police interested in my friend's visit. Led them to connect it with what I did to Marilyn and to wonder if I had cause to kill her."

"I swear to God—"

"Oh, shut up. You didn't do it to *me*—I know that. You just liked the way the pretty cop listened to you. You wanted your little moment."

Di flopped back in her chair, her gaze vacant. A silence built. Ara, holding her hand, gently kneaded her fingers.

"Becca Lassiter," she then said in a tired voice, "is the woman you saw. We share a house. Marilyn and Becca were on a panel together, and Marilyn told a bunch of lies about the Scoring. Becca's—impulsive. She had to come here, make a nuisance of herself. I decided to teach Marilyn a lesson. End of story, except that someone else must have disliked Marilyn enough to have been inspired by my attack."

Her eyes blazed. "Thanks to this Frank person, I had to spill my entire private life into the police record. Why *is* he here, by the way? Did someone invite him?"

Cowards all, no one volunteered an answer. Frank's jaw tightened, and blotches of color grew on his cheeks, but he made no move.

"Frank's my roommate," Dodge finally said.

"That's Dicenzo's doing, not ours."

"Maybe you should take a walk, Frank," said Ara.

But Di wasn't finished. "This Frank person, I asked the chief to note, was right on the spot every time something happened. What if he sneaked in through Marilyn's window? Hid in her closet until she came back from the TC meeting? He knocks her down, goes back out the window, and finishes his powerwalk. The kid's arrival is a pure fluke, of course. A lucky break. Frank not only gets to see everything, he also satisfies the murderer's classic urge to revisit the scene of the crime. When the kid and Dodge go out the window, Frank's there. He nabs the license plate and all hail the hero."

During this recitation, Frank gaped at Di, his face imploring and tortured. When she was finished, she rounded on him. "The pretty cop's waiting for you, Frank. In Dicenzo's office. I hope she gets you good."

Her voice, throughout, had been clear and carrying.

114

Several dozen people had heard every word. By breakfast it would be all over the Center.

Di watched Frank flee, then turned back to Ara. "Sip?"

He handed her his glass, which she drained. Setting it on the floor, she stood and tugged at his arm. "C'mon," she said, her smile wicked. "Let's establish another alibi."

"That," breathed Jeremy when they'd left, "is one tough broad."

"I *hate* this Scoring," wailed Kate. "I keep having to feel sorry for people I basically can't stand. First Marilyn, now Frank.'

"Me too," said Stacia.

"I'm calling it a night," said Dodge.

"Me too," Stacia said again, and Dodge offered to walk her home.

They were alone in the elevator. He could hug me, Stacia thought. For comfort. Didn't I hug him after his night in the hospital?

But Dodge had something else on his mind. "My grandmother used to say that God helps those who help themselves. Was she quoting someone, do you know?"

"Mark Twain?" mused Stacia, whose degree was in American Literature. "No, Ben Franklin. It's probably in *Poor Richard's Almanack*. Why?"

"Just wondered."

"Franklin could be naughty. I've often thought—to my horror—that if he were alive today he'd write for Saturday Night Live."

"What's naughty about God helping those who help themselves?"

"Sly's a better word. He's making fun of the idea—or the crock—that we're all in God's omnipotent hands."

They had reached her door. His hand on the back of her neck, Dodge pulled her close, so suddenly her mouth struck his collarbone. "Keep your door locked," he said, and then he was gone.

His embrace, if that's what it was, had caused one of her front teeth to graze the inside of her lower lip. Tasting the salt of her blood, she wondered how much she really liked Dodge Hackett. Or knew him at all.

Chapter 21

"How's Frank?" Stacia asked Dodge at breakfast. "Back to his insufferably cheery self?"

"I left him sleeping, He must've had a late night—I didn't hear him come in."

They dropped it there, not wanting to discuss Frank or Di with the rest of Table Fifteen, which was breakfasting together to celebrate the final day of the Scoring. It was cold in the dining hall. The tall, none-too-clean windows showed a pale gray sky fading to white at the horizon. A northeast wind whipped the long yellow branches of the willows that bordered the scruffy lawn.

"Looks like snow," Ellie Ostergard decided.

"Just pray it holds off," said Miss Brandt, yet to be called Joyce by any of them, "until we're safely home."

Safely home. Dodge and Stacia looked at each other. Except for that one outburst, Miss Brandt had floated impassively through the Scoring, her brisk reading pace unaffected by Marilyn's death. Apparently, though, she drew the line at snow.

Francie Squires was deep in *The Boston Globe*, with Mark Agresti looking on from one side and Joe Callahan the other. The entire dining hall in fact, bloomed with open papers. This was unprecedented. Normally, once the hermetic nature of the Scoring had fully asserted itself, hardly anyone bothered to order the morning paper. But of course this year, and particularly this morning, the news was urgently relevant.

Media people and camcorders, yesterday, had been thick on the ground. Francie alone, as the co-scorer of Jason's essay, had been interviewed by five reporters—two print and three TV. Last night, on the ten o'clock local news, she had communicated concern and her own considerable physical charm. Dodge, who'd missed the broadcast, had yet to find anyone sufficiently struck by her words to recall them. Now, her expression wry, she lowered her *Globe*. "It says here that I 'seemed obviously distressed.' Well, that's fair enough."

"They spell your name right?" Bob Gorman asked in his arch, possibly sneering, way.

TCs have to rise above it, keep the peace. Francie gave Gorman's remark a light laugh and attended to Ellie, who wanted to know if there was anything new on Marilyn.

"They interviewed her mother, who lives in Massapequa, if that's how you say it, New York,"

"Mass-a-PEE-kwa," corrected Miss Brandt.

"Thanks. It says she's a stylish widow."

Gorman snickered. "That's journalese for overaged sexpot. We may have a dissertation subject here. Famous feminists spawned by sexpot moms."

"My sons," Ellie mildly offered, "consider themselves feminists."

"Faute de mieux," Gorman murmured, imagining, from the look of him, that he'd achieved wit at sturdy, clean-scrubbed, Ellie's expense.

" 'I've always been proud of my daughter,' " Francie read, " 'though I can't really say I share her view of society today.' "

" 'Society today.' " Mark Agresti said. "I wish I had a dollar for every essay I've read that started out with 'society today.' "

" 'My daughter,' " Francie continued, " 'felt that teaching was a sacred trust. If it was against the rules to contact students, she would not have contacted anyone. Someone is lying. Someone wants to blame the victim.' "

"Interesting theory," said Agresti, who, naturally, knew nothing yet of the postcard Marilyn had sent to the boy in Texas. Would Rasene, Dodge wondered, announce this development later in the morning?

"Read them this," Joe Callahan said to Francie, pointing to the page opposite.

"It's a related article," Francie said, "on the C.A.T.s in general. Admissions spokespersons at Harvard, Yale, Cornell—did you guys know Marilyn did her graduate work at Cornell?—and Wellesley 'readily admit to serious doubts,' blah, blah, blah. 'We are well aware'—this is the one from Yale talking—'that students have earned high scores simply by regurgitating memorized essays revised by cram schools. The C.A.T. people have never been—' "

She broke off and made a face at Callahan.

" '—sufficiently rigorous about essays that are not quite on topic,' " Callahan triumphantly finished.

Throughout the Scoring, Francie had refused to let Table Fifteen punish the cookie-cutter World War II papers that had popped up with suspicious frequency. There'd be an introductory sentence in authentic Kidspeak: *Society today is chained by blatant militarism in world affairs.* This would be followed by three mechanically acceptable paragraphs about the origins of World War II, followed by a Kidspeak conclusion clanking with more tacked on chains. Callahan had concocted a series of legitimate-sounding topics that could be illustrated by the origins of World War II. Francie had been amused but refused to budge from the official C.A.T. position. Essays are scored on their individual merits, period. If most of the sentences are clearly expressed and mechanically sound, it's going to be at least a three.

Stacia, who'd rather listen to anything than more of Callahan's futile argument, asked if that was the end of the article.

"No indeed," said Francie. "Next comes the usual rehash, the C.A.T.s favor the white middle class, blah, blah. Professor Allan Bloom—is anyone else as sick of him as I am?—puts in his usual two cents for educational rigor but withholds full endorsement of the C.A.T.s. However, the tests get a ringing defense from Dr. Prescott Beasley—'the North Shore patrician who long ago loaned his ancestral acres to this enterprise.' "

"Loaned?" Callahan asked. "I thought this place was forever."

"My understanding is that the ancestral acres are bequeathed," said Dodge.

"Closing quote comes from—ta-ta!—our very own Cliff Rasene. 'Everyone involved has bent over backwards to keep this tragic event from interfering with or in any way invalidating our important work.' "

Ellie beamed at her tablemates. "Doesn't Cliff do us proud!"

Gorman yawned. "Any mention of Di Royce?"

"No, but why would there be?" Francie asked.

Gorman gave a short laugh. "Obviously you don't consider her the starting point for this whole tragedy."

"Obviously not," Francie imperviously agreed.

"Is there anything about Mop-up?" asked Miss Brandt.

"Well, no matter. I, for one, have no inclination to volunteer this year. Especially when everyone has fallen so far behind schedule."

Everyone but me, she complacently meant. But only those whose backs were to the breakfast buffet paid any attention. The others sat transfixed as Frank St. Leger, eye swollen nearly shut, three dark scratches raked down to a split, puffy lip, moved haltingly toward a near-empty table.

Dodge intercepted him. "What happened, Frank?"

"First let me put this stuff down."

"Sure. Got all you need?"

Frank produced a wan laugh. "Maybe too much. Eating's going to be some fun with this lip."

They sat across from the three southerners Jason had observed waiting for their night of Route 1 sin. So voluble were these stalwarts, so outraged at what decent, law-abiding folk had to endure in this day and age, that Dodge had difficulty sorting out the story.

When Chief Trevor had finished with him—all she'd wanted, Frank said, was to go over his story again, make sure he hadn't left anything out—he had grabbed his coat and gone outside to cool off. The stars, thick and bright, had promised the healing balm of the cosmic. To escape the interference of the Center's lights, he had walked some distance down the dark driveway.

"It was either a medium-sized boy or a pretty big girl. Came out of the shadows and bashed me one."

"Wait a sec, Frank," said Dodge. "You mean boy and girl literally?"

"I figure it's a copycat thing. Some other kid pushed to the breaking point by C.A.T. pressures."

"What were you hit with?" asked one of the southerners.

Frank wasn't sure. "Could've been a baseball bat. Or a fallen branch."

"A two by two," said the southerner with an authority that bespoke frequent Saturday trips to the lumberyard.

"Maybe. I never saw it. Or a face to recognize." Another wan laugh, tightlipped to save the split. "What I saw was stars. With a vengeance."

"Now that's a good one," said the first southerner. "Get it, boys? Seeing stars?"

"Jesus, Frank," said Dodge. "Did you pass out?"

"I must have, because I don't remember collecting these scratches. I got damn cold, I know that." He ate a mouthful of scrambled egg, chewing carefully. "You didn't hear me, Dodger? I had to thaw myself in the shower."

"I didn't hear you."

"Hey! Lighten up! At least I'm here to tell the tale. Not like poor Marilyn."

"What in the world, Frank?" It was Cliff Rasene, trying to sound humanly concerned instead of furious at this latest affront to his Scoring. And Mop-up! *What about Mop-up?* Would anyone, after this, dare to come?

"It's my own fault, Cliff. I never should've gone out alone."

Rasene sat heavily. "Give it to me from the beginning," he said.

On the way to the phone to call Prescott, Dodge was bombarded by theories and questions from his agitated colleagues. First Marilyn, now Frank—was there a connection? Or had Frank been simply a random victim, caught in the wrong place at the wrong time? Meaning that anyone—*anyone!*—could be the next target? What if someone was trying to undermine the C.A.T.s by making the Center seem out of control? *Was* it out of control? Hadn't Di Royce gone after Frank as well as Marilyn?

Begotten violence with violence? Di's a friend of yours, Dodger, what do you think? Has to be more than coincidence, wouldn't you say? Wait! What if they infiltrate the kitchen? Oh my *God*. What if they go after our *food*?

"What's to stop them?" asked a grim Californian who would not, given distance, be expected to return for Mopup.

At length, Dodge made his call. Tank answered and explained that he'd spent a guardian night at the cottage.

"Gramper's in the tub," he then said. "Soaking his rheumatism. God, it's awful to be old."

"How's his state of mind this morning?"

"So-so."

"Maybe it's best if you tell him why I called. That way you can pick your time."

Filled in on Frank, Tank matched the southerners for shock and outrage.

Dodge waited for him to subside, then asked him to make sure Prescott called Jason's lawyer as soon as possible.

"Teddy? What's Teddy got to do with this? St. Leger wants to sue?"

"No, no. Jason's hearing is tomorrow."

"So?"

Why was the man being so dense? "Whoever attacked Frank, it wasn't Jason. My feeling is, the kid genuinely regrets the trouble he's caused—not just to himself but to other people. So if Teddy tells him someone new has been hurt maybe it'll unlock his mouth. Maybe what he's hiding will lead somewhere useful. Useful to all of us. Don't forget, we've still got Mop-up to get through."

"Wait. What's Julia going to say about this?"

"She might be trying to call Prescott right now."

"Doubt it. She flew to Philadelphia this morning."

Harkness College, where Marilyn had taught, was just

west of Philadelphia. "Doesn't she have to be on hand for Jason's hearing?"

"You know as much as I do," Tank said, and they hung up.

Chapter 22

Sunday was only a half day. After lunch the Readers would leave for home.

The last coffee break of the Scoring, always an intensely social interlude, was especially so this year. They had shared—No! Were sharing still!—great danger. The noise level, as speculations on Frank's beating flew back and forth, grew deafening. Great quantities of home addresses and phone numbers were scribbled. Promises to keep in touch felt unusually and poignantly genuine. Those who soon would meet again at the conference of the Modern Languages Association felt they could hardly wait.

Some people, murder notwithstanding, had spent part of the Scoring in bed with each other. Exactly as in calmer years, the couples whose lustful yearnings had led to happy satisfaction and a minimum of guilt stood close together, sipping their coffee in quiet reflection. Dodge had stood this way with Kate the year before her marriage. Other couples, the ones who had tried to make love and ended up with war, were hidden today within the general din. In calmer years, they revealed themselves by staying the hell away from each other, each half putting up a showily vivacious front.

This year, only Ara was quietly sipping. Di was laughing and chattering a bright blue streak, talking at rather than with her lover.

Dodge was trying to come to some conclusions about this change when Francie interrupted, telling him Mrs. Dicenzo wanted to see him.

"Now? What about the Scoring?"

"A few minutes won't make that much difference." Francie grimaced. "Mop-up's going to last past New Year's anyway. Assuming anyone shows for it."

Jeremy joined them. "Saw you on TV, Francie."

"My fifteen minutes of fame."

"Someone mentioned that you and Marilyn had sat side by side at the TCs preliminary. And I wondered—did you happen to notice her doing a lot of writing along with her reading?"

"TCs write all the time, Jeremy. You have to keep track of where you are with the model papers and all. You'll see how it works next year. Which reminds me, congratulations on making TC."

"Thanks. But hang in on this for a minute. You know how sometimes you'll be reading away, and your peripheral vision catches your seatmate doing something peculiar? One year a guy was keeping tally of Vietnamese names and how they scored. Wanted to write a paper, he said. Got all upset with me when I told him that was a strict no-no. You publish anything, I'll see that you perish, I finally had to say. Peripheral vision, right? This morning, the Reader who sits next to me—she's new this year—happened to say that I must have a phenomenal memory. Why's that, I said, and she said that when Marilyn was their TC she often stopped to write stuff down. Since I didn't do that, I must have a phenomenal memory. So what I wondered, Francie, was if you had caught Marilyn doing too much writing. Back at the TCs preliminary.''

''If I had thought Marilyn was up to something,'' Francie said, ''I'd have checked it out. I'd have spoken to her.'' She cocked a hip, decorated it with her fist, and lifted her face to Jeremy's. ''Wouldn't I?''

Uh-oh, thought Dodge. She should have stopped while she was ahead.

Jeremy, too, had heard a pleading falseness. He gave Francie a lazy smile.

Francie didn't smile back. ''If you have ideas concerning Marilyn's death you should tell the police, Jeremy. Not me. Nothing to *do* with me.''

She turned on her heel and marched away.

Jeremy watched her go, shaking his head. ''Great ass, huh, Dodge? And super-great legs. Assuming the sight of them hasn't totally wiped out your reasoning capacity, what do you think Marilyn was writing?''

Dodge wanted to tell about the postcards so badly he could taste it. ''Notes, I guess. But about what, who knows?''

''Francie, maybe.''

''Nah. Look how she reacted just now. She was hardly aware of the scribbling until you forced it on her.''

''Should I tell? Get her grilled by the chief?''

''What would that accomplish?''

Jeremy nodded. ''Back off, you're saying, ask the process question. What's my goal? Basically I want Francie extremely convinced that this QN is watching her for TN indicators. As a TC—you drowning in this alphabet soup?—I have a chance to make an impact on an important corner of this country's educational system. I'll be looking for notes, especially from other TCs of color. And a chain, I read in an amazingly good essay just this morning, can only be as strong as its weakest link.''

"Francie's a weak link?"

"Let's say she's inclined to go along to get along. But I won't tell on her. Not unless my warning fails to warn."

People had begun to file back into the ballroom. "For an aspiring man," Jeremy continued with a sigh, "a TN can be a real drag. If I don't see you before we split, have a great year."

"You too, Jeremy."

"You on for Mop-up?"

"Wouldn't miss it. Stacia's coming too."

"Take care, then. No moonlit strolls."

Jan Dicenzo looked drawn and tired. "Two more parents have called to say their kids got postcards," she told Dodge. "The crew and I were up most of the night, and we think we've found all the essays Ms. Milledge scored at the preliminary. She was a fast reader, which didn't help. We've reached most of them, and five got postcards."

"That's eight in all. No, nine. Have to count Jason, right? What about the essays Marilyn read in the Scoring proper?"

"That's next. Sufficient unto the day is the evil thereof. I made transcriptions of the postcards and copies of the essays. Dr. Beasley wants you to read them."

"Fine. First though, what kind of reaction did people have to your calls?"

"One dad threatened a lawsuit. Mostly people started out upset, but after I told them none of this had any bearing on their kid's score, they calmed down. Of course, when the acceptances come in, or don't come in, I should say, they might not stay calmed down."

"Well. Sufficient unto the day."

"I appreciate that, Mr. Hackett. Thank you. This whole

nightmare—I'm hoping God won't get tired of the sound of my voice."

She's born-again too, Dodge realized. She stayed up all night for the sake of a fellow believer.

"The top one," she went on, handing him a pile of photocopies, "went to the boy with the lawsuit dad."

Dear Mr. Wax: Dodge read. *I have read your response to the Rousseau paraphrase. You seem to me like the rooster (I borrow from George Eliot) who believes the sun rises only for the pleasure of hearing his crow. Sincerely, Marilyn P. Milledge, Ph.D.*

"Is that as insulting as I think?" Mrs. Dicenzo asked.

"It's pretty insulting." Dodge turned to the next page.

Dear Ms. Hanify: I have read your response to the Rousseau paraphrase. You should contemplate some lines from "Lady Windermere's Fan," by Oscar Wilde: "In this world there are only two tragedies. One is not getting what one wants, and the other is getting it." Sincerely, Marilyn P. Milledge, Ph.D.

"Cryptic," said Dodge.

"She must have liked that idea, because the next two are identical."

Dodge read them over to make sure, finding no variation except that both were addressed to young men. The next card was friendlier.

Dear Ms. Wingate: I have read your response to the Rousseau paraphrase. I congratulate you on your feminist awareness. Do read Charlotte Perkins Gilman. "There is no female mind," she once said. "The brain is not an organ of sex. As well speak of a female liver." Sincerely, Marilyn P. Milledge, Ph.D.

"That one's mom told me she and her daughter felt the card was a real honor," Mrs. Dicenzo said. "Takes all kinds, doesn't it?"

Dodge agreed and read on. *Dear Mr. Kraus: I have*

read your response to the Rousseau paraphrase. You make large claims for your own intelligence, but I find scant evidence of its operation. I remind you that "genius is an infinite capacity for taking pains." Your essay takes no pains at all. By the way, this familiar and valuable definition was coined by a woman. You seem unaware that the thinking world is occupied by anyone other then men. Sincerely, Marilyn P. Milledge, Ph.D.

"The woman's a walking Bartlett's," Dodge said.

"Bartlett's?"

"Book of familiar quotations. Also, look how every card begins and ends the same way. Peculiar."

Dear Mr. Barstowe: I have read your response to the Rousseau paraphrase. "Blessed is the man who, having nothing to say, abstains from giving in words evidence of the fact." (George Eliot). And surely you must know that God helps those who help themselves (Benjamin Franklin). Sincerely, Marilyn P. Milledge, Ph.D.

Eureka, thought Dodge, turning immediately to Barstowe's essay. Sure enough, there was that born-again hyphenation of God, a kind of tic interrupting what proved to be a vacuous gust of religious platitude. Reading, in the absence of paragraph breaks or transitional phrases, was difficult. Nevertheless, when Dodge came to the end he was confident that the hapless Barstowe had failed to produce a single line of substance.

But Dodge treasured Barstowe's every boring syllable. Now he knew what to say to Jason when he saw him later today.

He read quickly through the others, including the one written by the Texan with the four-by-four. *Plus which, if ever it snows, this boy won't be hassled by chains. (Joke)* Aside from young Wingate's, the essays were singularly inept—the kind of writing that makes English teachers wish they'd chosen an easy profession like neurosurgery.

Reading them, bludgeoned by their bland stupidities, Dodge felt spookily close to the impulse that must have led Marilyn to write her cards, to talk back, to slap these pinheads with some home truths.

Barstowe's essay, arguably the worst of the lot, could have cranked Marilyn up, inspired her first revenge. Jason's much better effort might have followed soon after. If so, Jason had been dosed with Barstowe's medicine less because he deserved it than because Barstowe deserved Kalaka at the very least.

Then Dodge had to go and tell the poor kid that God helps those who help themselves. Well, spilt milk. Dodge now knew what to say. That was the main thing.

Just conceivably, Marilyn's use of quotations, her formulaic beginnings and endings, were her way of concealing from herself the seriousness of her breach of confidentiality. But you had to wonder how tightly wired the woman had been. Less loony, she'd have found release from Barstowe and his ilk in fantasy, mentally scrawling hate letters while waiting for sleep. Kind of thing Dodge, any normal person, did all the time.

Or at least summoned the self-preservation to send the goddamned things out anonymously.

Chapter 23

The Scoring was over, its mission gravely incomplete. Also incomplete, down to half strength, in fact, was the roster of Readers who were still intending to return for Mop-up. Dozens had dropped out just this morning, Frank's beating the last straw.

Rasene's traditional farewell address was a plea for Mop-up recruits. Making it, he stuck to his decision to keep Marilyn's postcards secret. "No one in this ballroom," he announced, trying to sound jocular and upbeat, "needs to be told that the C.A.T.s Board is careful with money. Nonetheless, I have been authorized to pay the air fare of Readers who live beyond driving range and east of the Mississippi. We have a great deal of work ahead of us. Your support is urgently needed. May I have a show of hands?"

A reluctant few slowly complied.

Frank St. Leger was on his feet. The Readers caught their breaths. "I'd be flying from Minneapolis. If you're willing to call that east of the Mississippi, I'll be glad to come."

"Thank you, Frank. Thank you very much. Well, people? Who else?"

For a long moment the Readers hung between shame and anger. Frank, more than any of them, had cause to cower fearfully at home. But how dare the man reproach them with his courage? How dare he put them on the spot like this?

Shame won. A sufficient quota, drivers and flyers alike, answered the call. Ara, Jeremy and Kate did not. At Table Fifteen, Agresti and Callahan, muttering fiercely about Paper C and emotional blackmail, raised their hands. Miss Brandt, hanging tough, kept hers primly folded. Gorman, too, declined to answer the call.

"Maybe I should," Ellie fretted.

"Never," said Francie, exempt as a Californian. "Mothers do Christmas, and that's enough."

* * *

Dodge and Stacia had exchanged phone numbers and were saying goodbye in the lobby.

"I'm lousy at transitions," he told her.

"Me too. Are you really going to stay here tonight? All alone in this big ark?"

"Want to keep me company?"

"What do you mean?"

"Stick around. Play Nora to my Nick."

Right after breakfast, Dodge, on an impulse he didn't stop to examine, had told Stacia that Prescott had hired him, for twice his daily Center honorarium plus expenses, to visit Cornell. She'd asked how come. "He doesn't trust Julia Trevor's grasp of the academy," Dodge had parried. "And?" Stacia pressed. Dodge explained that there was a chance someone in Marilyn's past knew something that would lead the police beyond their insistent focus on Jason. "Which," he added, "has begun to strike Prescott as expedient." Stacia had given him a hard look. "What are you so carefully not telling me?" Still obeying his original impulse, Dodge had sworn her to secrecy and told the rest—the appalling implications of the postcards and Prescott's desire to redeem this betrayal of Center ethics.

Nick and Nora. A little joke. Stacia acknowledged it with a little laugh.

Now Dodge knew why he'd spilled beans to her. He'd needed to rehearse, to walk through his new role in front of an audience reliably safer than those waiting ahead. "You consider me laughable as a detective?"

Startled, she became serious too. "Not at all. You're good at seeing through surfaces. People like to talk to you. Assuming one of us killed Marilyn, and assuming relevant clues are hidden out there in academyland, you'll certainly find them before Chiefie-poo does. She's not too bright, you must have noticed."

"I have."

"I withdraw 'Chiefie-poo.' As Proust says, contempt is our natural revenge on harm we're powerless to prevent."

"Harm? What harm?"

"That which arises from her beauty." Stacia traced a delete sign in the air to change the subject. "Agresti thinks the person who beat up Frank is in Jason's church."

In terms oddly close to those Tank had used earlier, she explained why.

"You think that's plausible?" Dodge asked when she'd finished.

"Look at these people," she invited him, indicating their milling colleagues. "Are they plausible criminals?"

"Would you rather it turned out to be Jason?"

"Of course not. Poor kid. I wonder how he's doing."

"I'll find out this afternoon. Tomorrow, after Jason's hearing, I'm off to Cornell. Prescott casts a wide net. Turns out he's some kind of cousin of the head of the English department."

"Will you go to Harkness?"

"Not sure. I think the chief's there now."

Stacia looked at her watch. "I've got to run."

"You're not tempted? The first Jewish Nora?"

She gave him an urchin grin and a quick sock on the arm. "Call me if you're in New York," she said, and was gone.

A different guard was on duty. Luis Machado, his name tag said. He had a mustache lush as Ara's and kind, sorrowing eyes that seemed glued to Dodge's doughnut.

"Cracked my tailbone," Dodge told him. "Where's Jason?"

"He no come out. His mom here before, he no come out for her."

"Will you take him a note for me?"

"No problem, sure."

Dodge found a fresh page in the small notebook that he'd purchased, with great self-consciousness, for his detective work. *Dear Jason,* he wrote, *I'm sorry if I seemed flip or careless last night. What I said was something my grandmother used to say to me, and she was a religious woman who—*

No. Lay it on a bit. He turned the page and started again. *. . . a faithful churchgoer who said grace before every meal. So I thought it was an okay thing to say. I was wrong. Professor Milledge was wrong, very wrong, to have made a similar kind of mistake with you. And of course she should never have communicated with you in the first place. Please don't judge me by her. I believe in your innocence and I want to help you. With great concern, Dodge Hackett.*

Torn out and folded in half, the note looked like something a kid would sneak another kid under Teacher's eye. He passed it through the steel mesh to Luis, adding a five-dollar bill. "That's for your trouble, Luis."

The man thanked him and was soon back. "He take, but he no come out."

"Did he read the note?"

"No. He put in pocket. He read soon. He read everting."

"People have been writing to him? Keeping in touch?"

"For sure. His mom bring cards, many, many cards." A white and gold smile. "Bible too. Hoo! That boy read Bible for *sure*."

"He still in a cell by himself?"

"No more."

"Jeez. What's the other guy in for?"

"Arm robbery."

"Big guy? Hard?"

"No big. Hard for sure."

"When are you off duty, Luis?"

133

"Me? Midnight."

Dodge wrote down Prescott's number and extended it with another bill, a twenty. "If Jason changes his mind about seeing me, this number will work. Maybe you could kind of watch over him and remind him I'm hoping to hear from him? Mention it every now and then?"

"OK," Luis said, accepting his payoff.

Dodge waited for some claim of vigilance or guarantee of Jason's physical safety. "He'll be all right, Luis?"

For answer, a *quien sabe* shrug.

"Can I—?" Dodge indicated his open wallet.

Luis shook his head, lifting his palms to push away the proposal. Jason, apparently, would have twenty dollars worth of protection. Unable to give more, Luis, a man of honor, would not take more.

Chapter 24

Driving west in the compact that Tank Beasley had rented for him, Dodge couldn't stop thinking about Jason's arraignment. Its briskness had shocked him, the whole process absorbing less than a half-hour of the court's time. The facts—Jason had fled the scene of a capital crime, twice violated parole, and committed recidivist car theft— were laid out by an Assistant D.A. Then it was Teddy Massack's turn. Being locked up for a night with a brute had not frightened Jason into confiding in his lawyer. Lacking hard facts Teddy was obliged to fall back on the soft, pleading his client's previously blameless career as parolee, supermarket bagger, churchgoer and honor student. Clearly, Teddy told the judge, someone or something had terrified the boy, preventing him from cooperating in his own defense. Moreover, the Commonwealth had in no way accounted for last night's assault on a second teacher and Jason's patent uninvolvement in this crime.

The judge lifted a warning hand, and Teddy hastened back to the more relevant ground of Marilyn's postcards. "Jason Armbruster," he then declared in what his law partners called his million-dollar voice, "is a brilliant boy who was besieged by academic stress. On top of that, it seems unarguable that he was cruelly provoked by the deceased's flagrantly unprincipled action."

Knowing that Prescott would secure it, Teddy asked the judge to set bail so that Jason could return home and continue with his studies.

"If Jason wants bail," the judge said, "he can start by telling the court what he was doing at the side of the deceased."

Jason closed his eyes and began to pray.

Fed up, and having no other choice, the judge gave the Commonwealth what it had decided to ask for. Jason was charged with murder, second degree, and remanded—Dodge learned a new verb—to a DYS secure house until his trial date.

Outside the courtroom, pushing through the crowd toward Teddy, Dodge found his way blocked by a jubilant Jill Brower, the *North Shore News* reporter. "Storywise," she said, "the postcards are a dream come true. All I need now is the truth about the famous fight."

'What fight?''

"Please? Pretty please?''

"I've got to run. Teddy Massack's waiting for me."

He and Teddy found a corner where they could talk.

"Murder two is good," Teddy said. "Means the most they think they can get is manslaughter. Like, he went for her but didn't mean to hurt her so bad."

"How long before the trial?" Dodge asked.

"A month? It depends on the court backlog and how long it takes to put the cases together. Which for our team might be forever."

"You'll keep after him, won't you, Teddy? Call him every day?"

"I'll try."

"And maybe try to like him some? If only for Prescott's sake?"

Teddy's shrug was unapologetic. "Kid's a fanatic. You tell Prescott I did my best."

Was Jason a fanatic? Charged, he'd begun to cry. Not the broken sobbing of a scared and bewildered kid, face buried in his hands. These were proud tears, proffered upon cheeks taut with resolve, maybe even ecstasy. Dodge thought of El Greco's martyrs, eyes rolled heavenward. But should he marvel at the boy's piety or fear for his sanity?

Now, bound for Cornell, it was a question he continued to ponder. Like Marilyn, Jason might not be wired too tight. On the other hand, he might be incredibly strong, sustained by a genuine and living faith. Worst would be strong and crazy together—like Courtney. Strong and crazy and potentially suicidal.

It had taken terrible strength for Courtney to throw herself in front of that train. To deliberately choose the 7:43, which her parents rode every morning to pursue their almighty careers in arbitrage or whatever it had been.

Not a good road subject, teen suicide. Dodge switched to what Prescott had told him about Chief Trevor's trip to Harkness College. Apparently nothing had turned up that had any bearing on the murder. Marilyn Milledge had been admired by her colleagues and the all-female student body. "Some of the girls," Prescott told Dodge, "spoke of loving her. I made some notes, let's see, where in Sam Hill, ah, here we are. 'She made us think,' 'She gave fantastic lectures.' 'It's great how famous she was. Like you could be famous too.' "

Here Prescott had broken off. "Would you enjoy fame, Dodge?"

"For its lubricant value, sure. Otherwise not."

Prescott nodded. "Give me privacy. Any day."

Marilyn's privacy, Prescott went on, her papers, bills, letters, checkbook, had revealed nothing of interest. "Julia was quite short with me. She hopes I'm satisfied. She is satisfied. She's sorry that Miss Milledge's postcards have put the Center in the wrong, but enough's enough, she said. Apparently Detective Connolly accused her of trying to kill the Commonwealth's case."

"How was she doing that?"

"Her trip to Harkness for more evidence carries an implication that she's dissatisfied with what the Commonwealth has."

"Sounds to me as if Connolly might be a tad dissatisfied too."

"That's exactly what Teddy Massack said. I'm glad you're going to Cornell. I hope I'm paying you enough."

Dodge assured him that he was. Especially—he didn't mention this part—since he had nothing else pulling at him, certainly nothing as intriguing as the puzzle of Marilyn's murder. His inquiries might even prevent him from having to spend Christmas with Diana and Bud, his mother and current stepfather.

Not far from the New York line, the snow that Ellie Ostergard had predicted for yesterday began to fall. As if compensating for tardiness, it hit hard—wet, sloppy flakes that loaded the compact's undersized wipers and steadily narrowed Dodge's view of the highway.

Spotting a Best Western motel, he decided he'd had enough and pulled in. After eating their idea of a rare burger and garden-fresh salad, he undressed and lowered himself into a hot, deep tub.

His ass hurt more than yesterday, partly from driving but also because he'd been too shy to bring his doughnut into the hotel restaurant. Relaxed now, he vowed an end to such hesitations. He was a detective, not a self-conscious lad of fifteen. And what's a detective without a schtick?

Mr. Donut, then—and *proud*.

Chapter 25

Dodge presented himself to Henry Trumbull, Chairman of Cornell's English Department, just after lunch. With a burdened air, Trumbull scanned Prescott's letter of introduction. "This is a terribly busy time," he began, breaking off when his eye locked on the doughnut. A complex expression crossing his face, he invited Dodge to sit down.

Dodge told him about Jason's arraignment, then, modesty to the winds, said that he'd come to Cornell because he was Jason's last, best hope. "And as you see, Prescott's solidly behind me."

"Dear old Prescott. Not quite of this world, of course. Never has been."

"I've brought two lists. One's the people who attended the Scoring, the other is everyone who works at the Beasley Center. What I'm looking for, of course, is a connection to Marilyn. A fellow student, former teacher, anything."

"Doesn't Prescott have everyone's academic background on file?"

"Just their most advanced degrees. The person I'm looking for could have come here as an undergraduate."

Trumbull pursed his lips. "I see. But as I said, end of term's an impossible time. You should have called to make appointments."

Detectives never call ahead, dummy. "I know. I'm sorry. I was hoping you could get me started by running these names through your computer."

"Can't do it. Not unless you have written permission from each and every one."

"Are you serious?"

"Perfectly. It's an unlooked-for result of the Freedom of Information Act. We had a divorced father call the other day. He wanted his son's transcript—apparently the son hasn't been entirely straight about his academic standing. I had to tell the father no dice. Seems less than fair, because he's had to pay for educational opportunities that his son essentially has wasted, but that's what the civil libertarians have saddled us with."

"How about Marilyn's transcript? Can I see that?"

"Not without permission from her estate."

Dodge couldn't stand it. Everything he wanted was within reach of a couple of keystrokes! "All right. I'll call Marilyn's mother and have her phone you."

"I'd need it in writing."

"An innocent kid has been wrongly incarcerated, Mr. Trumbull. There's no time to get things in writing."

"Sorry. I didn't write the law."

Dodge felt very young, very like a student being caught forging an absence note. Abandoning his hastily contrived plan to get Stacia to commit a phone impersonation of the stylish widow of Massapequa, he asked Trumbull if he would mind going over the lists himself.

Trumbull accepted them grudgingly but read the lists with apparent care. "Nothing," he then said, handing them back. "Of course, I'm notoriously poor with names."

"Did you know Marilyn well, Dr. Trumbull?" (Be sure, Prescott had warned, to call him doctor.)

"No more or less than any other graduate student. It was, what? Fifteen years ago?"

"When the department learned she'd been murdered, what was the reaction?"

"Really, Mr. Hackett. You remind me of a television reporter at a fire. 'What's it like, Mrs. Housewife, seeing your babies burn?' "

"That tough, huh? She must've had lots of supporters."

"I didn't say that."

"I heard babies and I assumed—well, who cares what I assumed. I was trying to find out if Cornell is proud of Marilyn."

"Cornell is a very large institution."

"Are you, then?"

"Am I what?"

"Proud of Marilyn."

"Let me be frank, Mr. Hackett. Marilyn Milledge was not an easy woman to work with. She was a contrarian— of a particularly determined sort. If you succeed in posing to other members of the English faculty the same kinds of questions you've been asking me, you will gather that some people were relieved when she finished her work here. I don't mean to imply that her degree was not fully earned. She shot her contrarian arrows from a solid bow. But she exhausted us, Mr. Hackett. She tired us out. If you talk to us, you may hear remnants of that fatigue. But you will not be encouraged by this to pester and harass. Is that clear? I won't have my faculty bothered, especially when we're coping with end-of-term work."

"I understand," said Dodge, all humble-pie. "Believe me, if I weren't worried sick about Jason I'd never press you like this. I wish you could have seen him there, in the dock. He's about five-seven, a hundred and twenty-five pounds. They get some rough kids at those DYS houses. Armed robbery, rape, homicide, drug dealing, you name it. Wait. I just had an idea. What if you give me the names of the people who knew Marilyn best? That way I can leave everyone else in peace."

The Chairman didn't like this. At length, though, he handed over the names of two men, Morton Kaslow and F. X. Finnerty.

"And now, Mr. Hackett—"

"Right, Dr. Trumbull. I'm history."

Kaslow wouldn't be out of his seminar until three, but Finnerty was holding office hours. Five students waited ahead of Dodge. Deadbeats. There to beg extension times on overdue work, probably. No one was improving the passing moments with an open book. That's how Dodge knew they were deadbeats.

"How's it going?" he asked the youth sitting next to him.

"Don't ask. You?"

"Not too bad, except for this thing."

No embarrassment from the kid. Too young, Dodge supposed, to know the many indignities flesh is heir to. "What happened?"

Two of the students wore headsets. The other two could

become an audience if they wanted: the more the merrier. "Cracked my tailbone. Where it happened might interest you—at the C.A.T. Scoring."

"Yeah? I thought they did that with machines."

"This was the essay part. We read about eighty thousand in four and a half days."

"Huh."

"I'm curious—do you remember your essay question?"

Brief pondering. "Something about heros?"

Last year's topic. The kid was a freshman—what Jason would have been this time next year if he hadn't fucked up. " 'Heros,' " Dodge quoted, " 'are made, not born.' ".

"Something like that. Hey! You could've read mine."

"It's possible. You must've done well, if you got into Cornell."

"Yeah, but you know? It's not worth it. College—I don't know, college isn't what I thought it was gonna be."

"What was that?"

"Huh?"

"What did you think you'd find here?"

"I don't know. Excitement. The hype—you know. I mean, all through high school—I went to this real intense private school. You know? Stress City."

"College is easier?"

"Basically. The pressure's off. No one gives a shit what you do."

"Your parents don't care? What's Cornell cost these days?"

"They can handle it." The kid's laugh revealed his angry belief that his parents were good for money and nothing else. "I don't know. It's like college is the end."

"The end of your formal education?"

"No, man. The *end*."

There is a gorge at Cornell, beautiful and deep. Slung

over the gorge is a footbridge. Academic lore has it that students, in the dark of the year, jump like fleas.

The door to Finnerty's office opened. The young woman who came out was weeping into a piece of purple tissue.

It was the turn of the kid Dodge had been talking to. "Wish me luck," he said, and disappeared into the office.

Left to wait, Dodge felt depression descend. America's throwaway kids. The ones in this room had been given more than most—more stuff, anyway. Call them purple tissue instead of plain white, they were throwaways all the same.

Chapter 26

F. X. Finnerty, it turned out, not only had taught Marilyn but also had advised her dissertation. "*Sainted Doormats*, she titled it. Women in modern Irish literature. Shrill in spots, which I chalked up to youth's natural excess. I've often wondered: by demanding revision then and there, might I have moderated what was to come?"

Once Dodge had explained why Jason had brought him to Cornell, Finnerty suggested drinks at his house, around six. "Mort Kaslow lives nearby, so he can come too. I owe him anyway. Actually, I owe Elaine—Mort's wife. She's cooked me many a meal since my own wife took off."

Before Dodge found a response to this, a wry smile relieved the harshly scored verticals of Finnerty's craggy face. "Ditched at midlife by a woman bent on self-realization. Marilyn would be pleased."

Having grown up on Boston's Beacon Hill, Dodge knew his Irish—pols and their bullyboys, ruddy of face, glad of hand. Finnerty was the other kind of Irishman. In the Age of Faith, he'd have launched a coracle and rowed off to some rocky, wave-beaten isle, his solitude sustained by prayer and dewdrops.

"By the way," Finnerty went on, "there's a young woman from Harkness here, working on her doctorate. Carla Jaeger. She's in my Yeats class. I'm no fan of Marilyn's, especially not the tabloid Marilyn, so I've never let on to Carla that I was her advisor. Of course Marilyn may have briefed Carla on me, but I gather not. Anyway, you might want to speak to her."

Dodge said he'd appreciate Finnerty's help in arranging a meeting.

Carla Jaeger, dark and intense, disconcertingly reminded Dodge of Stacia. They met in her landlady's sun porch, a chilly realm of sprung cushions, much-knuckled wax begonias, and ancient snake plants. A glass door away, in the cosy living room, the landlady watched a game show on TV.

"She always keep it that loud?"

"Yes. Look, I don't have much time. What exactly do you want to know?"

"I knew Ms. Milledge only by sight. Whatever you can tell me about her will help."

"Marilyn was the best thing that ever happened to Harkness."

"You used her first name. Is that a Harkness standard?"

This absurdity was greeted with a short laugh. "Titles are hierarchic, Marilyn said. Invented by men because they can't have babies."

Having no particular quarrel with the theory, Dodge nodded. "Why was she so good for Harkness?"

"Mainly because if she wasn't there, serious students would never go near the place. Women's colleges have enormous potential, but without gender awareness, the bubbleheads take over."

"If your idea of bubbleheads is the same as mine, it's hard to imagine them taking anything over."

Carla shrugged. "Path of least resistance. Look at network TV. That game show in there, the useless junk the ads keep cramming down our throats. Look at top-ten music, the top-grossing films and books. Of, by and for bubbleheads."

"I see your point. What about the Harkness faculty? How's their gender awareness?"

"Marilyn's done some good work with them."

"Did everyone like being worked on?"

"Of course not. College isn't about knowledge any more than law is about justice."

"What's college about?"

"Power. The older faculty still think power comes from copying the patriarchal establishment. History is wars and kings, literature is the writing of white western men. Bias and bullshit, Marilyn said. Empower yourselves, she told us."

"It's hard when someone starts yanking at the rug you've stood on all your life."

"So? You want the planet to survive or not?"

Declaring for survival, Dodge handed her his lists. After scanning them quickly she handed them right back, shaking her head.

"I know you're busy," he said, "but could you give it one more go?"

Instead of answering, she recited the first five names of the longest list. "Photographic memory," she explained, enjoying his astonishment. "Anyway, you can forget about Harkness. One thing the old guard hasn't co-opted from the mighty male is physical violence. That's for us young radicals, and all of us wanted Marilyn alive and fighting."

She broke off, stopped by a surge of grief. Her hero, her trusted mentor, was dead and gone.

"Shit," she said, bowing her head and scrubbing her eyes with a rough fist. *"Shit."*

"I'm sorry," Dodge began.

One arm hiding her tears, she chopped away with the other. Get out of my life, he read, and did, game-show frenzy pursuing him down the front stoop.

The encounter left him feeling empty, possibly hungry. Before going in search of Finnerty's house, he stopped at a college hangout to grab a burger and fries, counter service. "And a coke," he added, surprising himself. He hadn't touched the stuff for, what? Ten years?

Finnerty had changed to a ribbed sweater that hugged his lean, pared body. His living room was underheated and bare enough to evoke the cargo limitations of coracles. Instead of dewdrops, however, whiskey was offered.

Kaslow was already there. A more familiar type, Kaslow—stooped, rumpled, soft. "Victorian," he curtly responded to Dodge's question about his specialty. His fielding of further questions convinced Dodge that Kaslow was one of those academics far less interested in teaching than in staking out a patch of turf and defending it against all comers, students included. In the Age of Faith, Kaslow would have been a very different kind of monk from Finnerty—more on the order of the librarian in *The Name of the Rose*, hoarding to himself every scrap of manuscript.

What's college about?

Power.

Before Dodge could ask any questions, both professors

demanded full details of Marilyn's death. This occupied the first round of drinks, neither man bothering to dress his interest in fake sympathy or protestations that he'd liked the woman personally, objecting only to the flamboyance of her recent work. Finally, refills in hand, they were willing to move on.

Dodge described his frustrated attempt to utilize the university database and passed them copies of his lists.

This time, one bell rang. Kaslow remembered a student called Kenneth Cheatham. Black or white, Dodge asked, and the bell was extinguished. The professors gamely returned to their study of the lists, until Dodge, hoping to prime some lost pump, asked them what they remembered most clearly about Marilyn.

Kaslow spoke first. "She kept trying to redesign my syllabus. Nineteenth Century Novel, I think it was. Yes. 'Women hold up half the sky,' she'd say. 'They deserve half of our attention.' In the beginning, I humored her. It was the early seventies. Like most of my colleagues, I was glad to see attention focused on text for a change—instead of Vietnam and racism. But Marilyn was a pain. If the assignment was Scott, she'd keep interrupting to talk about Ann Radcliffe. That sort of thing. Then, to cap her career, she spread it around that I'd made a pass at her." He cocked an eyebrow at Finnerty. "F. X. remembers well. He was Acting Chair."

"A real pioneer, our Marilyn." said Finnerty. "Sexual harassment, as currently institutionalized, would not be invented for years."

Kaslow shuddered theatrically and went on. "The Chairman, Sawyer, was on leave, recovering from heart surgery. Thank God. Sawyer hated me. He'd have jumped at the chance to have my ass. With F. X. at the helm, the thing blew over fairly fast. Still. Unless it's happened to you, you can't understand the horror—*the horror*—of such an accusation.''

"It did happen to me," Dodge said. "Just once. The girl was a famous liar, so I survived.''

"What'd she look like?''

"The girl? Very pretty. Especially when she was lying.''

"Good bod?''

"Exceptionally.''

Kaslow nodded, satisfied. "Wait until a broad who looks like Marilyn accuses you of going for her. Wait for that, and then we'll talk horror.''

Dodge was on the point of asking Finnerty for his memories of Marilyn when Finnerty excused himself, saying he wanted to try to find something in his study. At length he returned, blowing dust off the top of an old-fashioned wooden file box. "I'd forgotten I had this. It's from my glory days as Acting Chair. I was very conscientious. My wife enjoyed being Mrs. Chairman. Enjoyment being a novel response for her, I began to hope Sawyer wouldn't recover. Anyway, here's a set of filecards I made on all the English majors—handy for writing recommendations and the like. Want me to flip through them? Read the names out to you?''

It didn't take long, Blodgett, Willard, occuring at the beginning of the alphabet.

Dodge couldn't believe it. Blodgett, the first to flee the Scoring. "Did people call him Will?''

"I don't know," said Finnerty. "I'm drawing a complete blank on the guy.''

Kaslow was staring at his copy of the list, where Blodgett was listed as Will. "Pale little fellow, buck teeth," he said, gradually remembering. "It was Browning and Tennyson.''

"Right you are," said Finnerty. "You gave him an A.''

"I did? Funny I didn't pick up on his name. Probably would've if he'd been listed as Willard."

"He took Browning and Tennyson his junior year," Finnerty said. "Says here he dropped out after that." Finnerty's boyish smile lit his face. "Guess who he had for Freshman Comp?"

All large universities utilize the optimistic, not to say naive energies of graduate students to teach composition, the most vexing course in the curriculum. The graduate student who'd taught Blodgett was Marilyn Milledge.

"Interesting," mused Dodge, working hard to keep his cool. He didn't want gossip exploding, tipping his hand. If the profs knew that Blodgett had skipped the morning after the murder, they'd be hard to hold.

He reminded himself that it didn't follow that Blodgett was the killer. Certainly, though, he was a man determined to keep part of his past secret. The police had made a point of asking everyone about the Readers who'd left early. If anyone had recalled that Blodgett had mentioned attending Cornell or knowing Marilyn, Chief Trevor would have gotten right onto it. Visited Cornell instead of Harkness. Subpoenaed the database, or whatever cops did.

He asked Finnerty if he'd mind going through the rest of his file, just in case. Finnerty obliged, but no one else turned up.

"What's Blodgett doing now?" Kaslow asked.

Dodge answered evasively. "I think he's at some prep school."

"Dreary work, prep schools," Kaslow said. "Make you nanny the kids around the clock."

"Any idea why he dropped out?" Dodge asked.

"Students did, then," Finnerty said. "Remember? 'I gotta do my own thing,' they'd say. They'd get into community organizing or voter registration. Or what used to be called exploring alternative life-styles. Different now. Mostly they charge straight through, grade-grubbing like fiends so they can get into law school. Always excepting, Dodge, those charmers you waited with this afternoon. When kids like that drop out, it's for academic reasons. Not like Blodgett, with his A in Browning and Tennyson.''

"If it turns out I taught him something that made him run,'' Kaslow said, rattling his ice, "I don't want to hear about it. Ever. Thank God he didn't jump. I haven't had a jumper for years, touch wood.''

Finnerty topped up their glasses. Dodge willed extra blotting power to his burger and fries. Whoever heard of a detective who couldn't hold his liquor?

"What will you do now?" Finnerty asked him. "Talk to Blodgett?''

"Not me. That's cop work. I don't even know how to find him.''

Kaslow shook his head. "You think of a killer, you don't think of a mousy little guy. Though of course she wasn't knifed or shot. Anyone mad enough could have grabbed her and given her a good shove. And the Marilyn I remember tended to attract violent response.''

"Positive as well as negative?" Dodge asked, thinking of Carla Jaeger.

"Oh definitely. No question about it.''

The talk moved to American violence in general, and, soon after, the gathering broke up.

Dodge drove with slow care, carrying his snootful safely to the motel Finnerty had recommended. It was too early to sleep, he didn't feel like eating, and the cable movie was one he hadn't liked the first time.

He sighed and reached for the phone, dialing Carla Jaeger's number. Sounding pissed off, she told him she was trying to write a paper and no, she'd never heard of Willard, or Will, Blodgett.

Skaneateles, he thought. Long one of his favorite American place-names, it was two Finger Lakes east of Cayuga and also Blodgett's hometown—a fact that had surfaced when Blodgett, referring to an essay that had mentioned the Underground Railway, had informed Table Fifteen that Skaneateles had been an important stop.

Dodge dialed information. Within fifteen minutes Blodgett's mother had told him everything he needed to know.

He stretched out on one of the huge beds—trust American motels to overdo the beds and skimp on the pillows—and let his mind drift. To Stacia, it turned out. During his long bike ride this fall, he'd broken two reveries like this by suddenly asking, What do I want to do right now; where do I want to be? The answer, with gratifying frequency, was Lie here until I fall asleep; ride my bike tomorrow. Now, surprising him as much as his earlier thirst for a coke had, the answer was Fuck Stacia.

Fuck her? How about calling her? By way of foreplay.

No. Calling her would be a mistake. She'd hear his excitement over Blodgett and demand to know what he'd discovered. Then she'd want to hear Chief Trevor's reaction.

Dodge, despite his promise, had no intention of communicating his plans to Chief Trevor. She'd barge right in, take over.

He was the one who'd found Blodgett. Blodgett was his.

Chapter 27

The boarders having left for Christmas vacation, Cheshire Academy, in western Connecticut, lay quiet under its postcard crust of snow. The night was windless but cold—lows near zero, the radio had said.

Dodge found a place to park within view of the corner of Mercer Hall where Will Blodgett had his ground floor housemaster's suite. The two windows in front showed light through their shades. A good reading light, it would be, at least a hundred and fifty watts. There'd be a comfy chair for Blodgett to tuck himself into with a drink and a novel. A spy story, or someone he was rereading. Dickens, possibly. Or Trollope, whose social intrigues would mesh well with prep school life. Come to think, Blodgett had told Table Fifteen that *The Eustace Diamonds* was one of the best mysteries ever written.

Shutting the car door carefully behind himself, Dodge took a deep breath and set forth over the crunchy snow. He felt bold and resourceful. He'd told Blodgett's mother that he was Mike Koutsopodiotis, a tongue-twister name meant to foil any impulse on her part to spoil Dodge's surprise appearance on her son's doorstep. Pretending to be an old classmate hatching a delightful surprise was, of course, a ruse inspired by the one Jason had used on Mrs. Ouellette. Mr. Donut took pleasure in this symmetry.

Blodgett's mother had been initially circumspect, if not

downright suspicious. "A classmate? From Cornell or Syracuse?"

"Syracuse," Dodge had said.

The right answer; Cornell must hold bad memories for her. Thawing immediately, she'd readily entered into the fun of helping Dodge surprise her son, whom she called Willard.

Three times during the afternoon Dodge had pulled over to check on Blodgett, hanging up as soon as the man answered the phone. By the third false alarm Blodgett had sounded irritated. And why not? This time of year, any housebound teacher was probably plowing through a stack of blue books or term papers. Grief enough without a pestering phone.

The nicely illuminated button on Blodgett's door generated a two-note chime. No answer. Dodge rang some more. Then he tried the door. Locked.

Dodge's imagination had written this scenerio: Blodgett, wearing slippers, shuffles to the door and peers out. He's like Ratty in *The Wind in the Willows*, braced for some grandiosity of Toad's that will completely trash his tranquil evening. He blinks—can't quite place Dodge. Next he's surprised, then, pell-mell, in sweeps the panic and dread.

So why wasn't he answering his door? Dodge's image of Blodgett as Ratty suddenly turned into Blodgett dead. Avenging himself on Marilyn had driven him to remorse, then suicide. He was in there right this minute, hanging by the neck, small feet adangle.

Paranoia, Mr. Donut scoffed. Blodgett was afield, not dead. His grading chores had left him snuffly and sleepy. He'd gone out for a brisk walk around the campus. Or he'd taken his car. Yes. There was the rectangle of bare asphalt where it must have been parked during the snowfall. He was having an early dinner. At worst, dinner and movie. It was just after seven; at worst he'd be home by nine.

Go looking for him? Dodge could use some chow himself. But where? Cheshire lay between two towns, and the highway offered more possibilities still. Blodgett could also be visiting friends. A married couple living nearby. Blodgett might be their housefriend—closer, in important and individual ways, to both than either was to the other, fond uncle to the kiddies. Housefriend was a role Dodge knew well, having enjoyed its multiple benefits often. Unfortunately, such triangles were short-lived. Possessiveness—the couple's, Dodge was pretty sure, more than his own—had a way of raising its ugly head.

Christmas was a stressful time. Blodgett, this exact moment, might be caught in some long-brewing connubial crossfire. Hard on him but excellent for Mr. Donut's purposes. Shaken and upset by the war between his friends, Blodgett would be an easier target.

Back in his car, Dodge stamped his feet and beat his thighs with his fists. He'd hold off on the engine as long as he could. At best, the compact's heater was cheapskate. Revving the engine enough to do any good would plume exhaust into the frigid night, alerting and forearming Blodgett when he finally showed.

At least he didn't have to worry about a watchman. To anyone braving the cold long enough to shine a flash in his face, Dodge would simply be in the neighborhood on business, hoping to surprise an old friend and hoist a few. The whole speech delivered with loud preppy heartiness. Benefits of background. Also of white skin. Cheshire, like most schools, doubtless had its "minority enrollments." Still, for a stakeout in this particular territory, white was right.

What if Jason had been black? Mrs. Ouellette might never have given him Marilyn's room number.

* * *

At eight, hallucinating a thermos of soup—black bean, fragrant with rum—Dodge decided. Five more minutes and the motor goes on. Before three minutes had passed, however, he saw the lights of an approaching car. It nosed into the oblong of bare asphalt. Dark, new and sleekly turbo, these were not the wheels Dodge would have predicted for Blodgett.

Even so, the man who got out acted like someone coming home, and Dodge moved fast.

Blodgett hadn't had time to take off his hat and coat. His hat, a war surplus, fleece-lined aviation helmet, suggested a certain playfulness. Like the sporty car.

As in Dodge's imagined scenario, Blodgett didn't recognize him until he hoisted his emblematic doughnut. "Dodge Hackett. I've been waiting for you."

Blodgett stood stonefaced, not moving aside or opening the door any wider.

"Man-oh-man," said Dodge, pushing past him, "that heat sure feels good."

"Why are you here? Cheshire's on vacation."

"Better shut that," Dodge said, keeping to his man-oh-man voice. "Down to zero, the radio said."

Blodgett shut the door. Dodge chose a Hitchcock chair with a Syracuse crest on the back. It was one of a matched pair. After a moment's hesitation, Blodgett took the other, behind a barrier desk neatly stacked with blue books.

"I wanted to ask you a couple of questions," Dodge then said. "I've just driven down from Cornell."

"I have nothing to say about Cornell."

"Would you rather talk to the police?"

"I've already talked to the police. I've done nothing wrong. I'm not remotely involved."

"Do the police know you were Marilyn's student freshman year?"

"I had no reason to mention it. Then or now."

"Let's review. At the end of Junior year you leave Cornell. Time passes. You finish your degree at Syracuse. More time passes, and you encounter Marilyn at the Scoring. One way or another, Marilyn gets herself talked about. Her fights with Cliff Rasene over Paper C, her tangle with Di Royce. But you never once let on that you knew her when."

"For the last time, she was nothing to me."

Instead of responding directly, Dodge took Blodgett through the events leading to Jason's appearance in court. "An innocent kid's been charged with murder and locked up," he concluded. "That bother you any?"

Straight and fierce on the edge of his chair, Blodgett's whole body trembled. "You have no right to hammer at me like this. I was with a friend from the time we all left the ballroom until well after the murder. The police know this and are satisfied."

Dodge grinned. "The Scoring's great, isn't it? Everyone who wants to can get laid."

Blodgett took his aimless flippancy like a punch to the midsection. He sagged back into his chair, the fight gone from him.

"Oh for Christ's sake, Will. We're all grownups. I don't care if you were screwing Prescott Beasley's dog. My job is to find out everything I can about Marilyn in the hope of saving Jason. My theory is he's waiting for God to call his next move. God keeping mum, it's up to the rest of us. The grownups, Will. We've got to try to save this kid from himself. Which is no big deal for a teacher, right? Don't you reach down and fish out sinkers every working day of your life? Course you do. Goes with the territory."

Blodgett looked sullen, cornered. "My relationship with Marilyn Milledge has no bearing here. None whatever."

"You can't be sure of that, Will. No one can be sure of anything at this point. Even the cops, I happen to know, aren't completely happy with their case. Don't force me to tell them—or to tell Jason's lawyer—that you and Marilyn go way back together.''

Hearing deal, Blodgett produced a thin smile. ''I will talk about Marilyn if you, as a gentleman, swear to lose all interest in where I was when she—'' Blodgett searched for the phrase he wanted ''—got hers.''

Chapter 28

The deal made, Blodgett wanted a drink. ''The Headmaster gives us all Johnnie Walker for Christmas. Just the thing for a stroll down memory lane.''

A jet of acid caromed around Dodge's stomach. He disliked Scotch; he wanted soup. ''Sounds great. Half tap water, please. And no ice.''

Blodgett began by describing Marilyn's effectiveness as a Comp instructor. ''She had an eagle eye for papered-over truths. Her comments were terrific. 'This recollection of a happy family gathering puzzles me,' she'd write. 'The mother is pathetically docile and self-sacrificing. Can children respond with joy to such a woman? Also, you say the father is powerful, but you don't show him doing or saying anything powerful. To me, he's a featureless blank, hardly there at all.' ''

Blodgett had to smile at the completeness of his recall. ''By the end of the term, I was writing honestly for the first time in my life. Producing very different kinds of stories. My mechanics improved too. I had something urgent to say and I wanted to give my ideas their proper due. I didn't want my readers distracted by misspellings or clumsy sentence structure."

He caught himself, embarrassed by his ardor. "Talk about people being in chains. Ever see a sculptural representation of Lincoln as The Great Emancipator? His hand resting on the head of a bowed and kneeling black man? It was like that with me and Marilyn. She freed me. I worshipped her.

"Sophomore year I began majoring in English. We got together evenings, weekends. We talked about everything. Books, music, politics, the men in her life—it won't astonish you that they were invariably inadequate—and my social backwardness. I was a late bloomer, she said. I had to give myself time. Meanwhile, why didn't I help her with some of her research?

"I'd never been so happy. I put her work before my own even after my grades started to slide. Someone—another English major—asked me was I getting credit for the work I did for her. You couldn't possibly understand, I told him."

He stopped talking and poured himself more whiskey. "You?"

"Just a touch. Thanks."

"Wait. You wanted water."

"No. This is fine."

"I'm not much of a drinker, you know."

"Now you mention it, I don't remember seeing you in the lounge very often."

"Would you call yourself a drinker?"

Blodgett's stalling had to mean the hard part was near. "I guess it's my drug of choice. The others are too boring or dangerous. But back to Marilyn—from what I heard at Cornell, they were glad to see the last of her. The Chairman said she wore them out."

"Yes. She would have. Still. Even now, after all that's happened, I can't—" He stopped and swallowed a couple of times.

Dodge hoped he wasn't going to cry. There were limits to Mr. Donut's toughness. "Did you keep in touch with her? After she started teaching at Harkness?"

"She called me that summer—I had my usual dipshit job at the hotel—and asked me to collaborate with her on an article. She was doing it on spec, of course, aiming for one of the scholarly quarterlies, she said. She wanted to analyze the course offerings of English departments all across the country. She hoped to find differences she could connect to regional socio-political currents. She wanted me to do the scutwork research—settle on the geographical distribution, collect the catalogs, work out a system of categories, stuff like that. This was before people like us used computers, so it would involve real drudgery. But so what? Collaborator! It was a dream come true. Well. You can guess what happened."

"You did most of the work and she took all the credit."

"That and worse. My categories included women and minority writers and what I called world writers—non-Western. It was striking how rarely these figured in the various curriculums. The women's colleges were doing the best job with them. Not the big-name women's colleges, but the little ones no one ever hears—Mohawk, for one, soon to attract Di Royce to its staff. Nice irony to that, huh? I told Marilyn it was as if these little colleges and my under-represented writers shared a kinship of the ignored."

"You coined that phrase? Amazing. Even in Winnetka teachers have been known to talk about the 'kinship of the ignored.' "

"I told Marilyn that we should forget about regional differences and concentrate on this other, far more impor-

159

tant and essentially unexplored issue. I pointed out that white men run the academy and decide what books should be studied. I said it was becoming clear to me that sexism, racism and imperialism in America are encouraged by this literary canon—by the thousands and thousands of syllabuses that, term after term, ratify attitudes congenial to the white male power structure. Books and writers are 'obscure' and 'marginal' because the establishment—male or crypto-male—finds them irrelevant to its values.''

"I'm impressed,'' Dodge said, meaning it. Whether one agreed or disagreed with these concepts, they had become, by now, integral to a great deal of academic discourse and curriculum planning. "This was what—twelve years ago?''

"The article came out almost exactly twelve years ago. Cover story in *The Atlantic Monthly*. Marilyn Milledge's career as a canon-basher and gender specialist was as well and truly launched. Willard Blodgett's name was not mentioned, a fact he learned only when, his hands shaking like spring leaves, he purchased a copy of the magazine at his neighborhood stationery store.''

"But this is incredible? Didn't you go after her?''

Blodgett waved a tired hand. "I called her. She offered a different version of things. True, I'd sent for the catalogues and arranged the findings into categories. But did I seriously think that clerical help warranted a mention? 'I didn't thank my typist, either,' she told me.''

"Jesus.''

"Yes. I went down to Harkness and tried to see her. She gave me five minutes—long enough to show me copies she'd made of a few stories I'd written for Freshman Comp. Frank, free investigations of youthful longings—hardly what someone aiming to embark on a teaching career would want circulated. Remember that this was a woman I had worshipped. My Great Emancipator. I ran to Mom and had a breakdown. After a couple of years in therapy I was still in no shape to try Cornell again, so I finished at Syracuse. My grandfather was a Cheshire trustee in the days when no one dreamed of appointing trustees for reasons other than financial. His generosity to the endowment allowed everyone to take a kindly view of my problematic past, and here I am. Cheshire's a second-rate school, just right for a second-rate man."

"Hey."

Another tired wave at this protest. "I know myself. Second-rate in every other respect, I am a first-rate writing teacher. Thanks, in part, to what Marilyn taught me back in Freshman Comp—the good stuff, I mean, not the spill-your-guts titillations. And I aspire to be a first-rate writer. Why not? Humankind cannot bear very much reality, as Eliot said. Aspirations help furnish the void. Did I mention I've recently sold a couple of short stories? Small-press, of course, but— Thank you. I'm rather pleased myself."

Before he left, Dodge had to ask it. "What did Marilyn do when she saw you at the Scoring?"

"Pretended she didn't know me."

"And?"

"I let her get away with it. Which cost me, of course. You must have noticed I was under a strain. No? What about the lilt in my step when Di Royce duked her out?"

"Mostly I wondered why you took off so fast."

"When Marilyn pretended she didn't know me, I quite literally wanted to kill her. It was like a slow-motion movie. I saw myself flying through space, hands braced to throttle the life out of her. If we'd been alone, I'd have gone for her. No question about it. So to find out that she was dead—that someone *had* gone for her, it was too rich, too much. The hours I had just finished spending with my friend had been exceptionally pleasant. For someone like me, when dreams start coming true, the guilt is crushing. Intolerable. I had to get out of there. I had to calm down."

Dodge, itching to find out whether the friend who'd given Blodgett such a pleasant evening, was, as he suspected, another man, nodded to show he understood.

Blodgett gave a short laugh. "I hope I don't need to remind you of our gentlemen's agreement?"

"Don't worry. As you kept trying to tell me, none of this is going to help Jason."

"I could have killed her."

"Yeah, but someone beat you to it."

"So where are you now? Sadder and wiser?"

"I'm no sadder than you that Marilyn can't steal any more ideas."

"Or mail any more postcards. You have to think, though. She might have done those kids a favor. Planted seeds in them that will grow into a healthy distrust of academic authority. As a college sendoff, what could be better?"

Chapter 29

When your mother is married to a man not your father, you lose crashing privileges at her house. Or so Dodge believed. And although his encounter with Blodgett had keyed him up so that he easily could handle the monotonous drive to Boston, he stopped instead at a motel near

Hartford. The kitchen about to close, he ate first—a surprisingly good steak, baked potato pooled with extra butter, spinach salad. Then, from his room, he made the call his mother might or might not be expecting.

In Chestnut Hill, the background noise was the eleven o'clock news, Bud's invariable ritual. Even so, mother and son had to give the lateness of the hour a few passes. Their invariable ritual.

"Am I still invited for Christmas?" Dodge finally asked.

"You're still *invited*. Of course."

"But?"

"No *buts*, darling. Good heavens. But Bud's kids are coming. I wish you'd let me know sooner."

Bud's kids were his tedious son and earnest daughter, each with spouse and small children of their own. A packed house. Yawns, forbearance and clamor. "Sounds like raincheck time," Dodge said.

"You know we'd love to have you. Now or whenever."

"I'll call if I change my mind."

They wished each other merry Christmas and hung up. For them, not too bad. He hadn't gone petulant, childish. She'd lied about wanting him, but in a nice way. Without any defensive anger.

Dodge knew that Prescott would be happy to hear from him, but better wait until daylight for that one. Who else? Stacia? Better wait on that one too.

Prescott, next morning, turned out to be full of news. "This Wax fella," he told Dodge, "the one whose son Miss Milledge likened to a rooster, has sued the Center. Countersue, our lawyer says—against Miss Milledge's estate. Much as I despise these maneuverings, fiscally speaking the Center has no choice. Then there's the matter of St. Leger's beating. Tank has been predicting lawsuit from that quarter as well. By the way, there was some suspicion that the fellowship was responsible—that they hoped to damage the case against Jason. Turns out, though, that the entire pro-Jason wing of the fellowship was occupied until midnight with a prayer vigil—for the boy himself, appropriately enough.''

"How is Jason?" Dodge asked.

"The same, I'm told. Says his prayers and not much else. I called his high school to make sure they're sending him his homework assignments. The director of that place he's in says he's not doing them, but I think it's important to keep the expectation alive, don't you?''

"Very important.''

"I sometimes catch myself admiring Jason's resolution. Then I remember what a godawful mess he's made of his life and I feel like an old fool. Speaking of which, nattering on like this I almost forgot—my cousin called me from Cornell. Claims he bent over backwards to help you. That so?''

In a spirit of all's well that ends well, Dodge said yes, Trumbull had helped. Then, first confessing that he had disobeyed Chief Trevor's injunction against independent action, he told Prescott the rest.

"Miss Milledge stole this Blodgett's entire theory?" Prescott asked after a pause. "Lifted it wholesale?"

"Without a word of acknowledgement. Public or private.''

"I can't believe it.''

"I can.''

"Yes of course. You were there. I mean that I can't bear it. A scholar who would— No. I cannot bear it.''

"Blodgett seemed pretty much of a cipher at the Scoring. But by the time we finished talking, I really liked the guy. He's a survivor. He went so far as to say he's indebted to Marilyn for teaching him how to write. The bad part is, everything I've learned is about Marilyn, not the killer. I hope you don't feel you have to tell Chief Trevor about Blodgett, Prescott. Since it turned out to be a dead end.''

"Rest assured. And thank you, Dodge, for taking the time to do all this. For humoring me, as Tank would put it.''

"I wasn't humoring you.''

"Thanks for that, too. Will you be with your family for the holidays?''

"I may go to New York. I'll put the car on my own tab.''

"Fine. Call again whenever you like. And Merry Christmas.''

Stacia answered on the fourth ring; Dodge was about to hang up. "Did I wake you?'' he asked.

"Yes, but I'm glad. Where are you?''

"Hartford. Look, some friends in New Jersey invited me for Christmas. How about I stop in New York first? Take you to lunch or something.''

"It's crazy out there. The shoppers and all. Come here. I hit Zabar's yesterday. You'll be saving me from solitary gluttony.''

He wrote down the address she gave him—her apartment and the closest garage. The friends in New Jersey, of course, were fabricated. You don't land on a woman you hardly know and say hi, my mother's busy with her latest family so here I am.

Expecting cramped, scholarly squalor, Dodge found a uniformed doorman, an immaculate marble lobby, more marble and fresh, expensive-looking wallpaper in Stacia's hallway. When she opened her door to him, his first impression was of polished wood, silk cushions, orientals that had to be real. A strong flat light filled the room. Its tall windows showed the Hudson River, silvered with afternoon sun.

Against this magnificence, Stacia, in black leggings and sweater, seemed a stranger. A sooty little smudge.

She was laughing at him. "My mother did the decorating."

"It's beautiful."

"It's Biedermeier. My grandparents had the wit to leave Vienna early, when you could still ship stuff. Come into the kitchen. Mom's Pierre Deux mode is easier to take. What've you got there?"

"Black bean soup, rum, and sour cream. Things I hallucinated on stakeout last night."

"Great. I've got lox and bagels. What do you mean, stakeout?"

"Am I astonished?" Stacia asked herself when Dodge finished his story. "Not very, I guess. Mostly I'm sorry I wasn't nicer to Will."

"You believe him, huh?"

"Oh yes. His eyes meet Marilyn's for the first time in twelve years. She pretends not to know him; he wants to kill. Someone steps in to do it for him. At breakfast Thursday morning—you were still in the hospital—Will was noticeably out of it. Not there. Gone before he was gone. Which fits. When something horrible happens to you, you feed yourself with revenge fantasies. People assume you're managing, getting over it, but inside, raging away, is this secret drama of confrontation and retribution. If the basis for that drama suddenly disappears, there's a hole. A big one. You're no longer the person you used to be."

Dodge knew, as clearly as if she'd said it, that she'd moved past Blodgett's wounds into some secret of her own. He thought of his drama with Courtney, his sense of rootlessness that morning in the Rockies when his guilt and remorse had eased; life without this burden had not yet begun. "A big hole," he said. "Yes."

Shoulders bent, Byzantine mouth soft and sad, Stacia spun her soup spoon around in its empty mug. "I've been here less than two years," she said, her voice low. "I used to live in the nineties, just off Columbus. That's what people who get paid like me can afford. I took the rats and roaches and neighbors' brawls in stride. Also the turds the winos left in the lobby. They had to shit somewhere, right? Nothing fazed me. I was living, with as little hypocrisy as I could manage, a life I'd consciously and freely chosen. Break-ins? Monthly at least. I prided myself they would never find anything worth fencing. The Biedermeier, of course, was in storage. The word would get around, I thought, that I had nothing. That I was one of them. Then, I thought, I'd be left in peace."

"The kinship of the ignored."

"Exactly. Then a guy broke in one night when I was home. Roughed me up. Scared me out of my principles. I let my parents move me. I let them pay and decorate. Nowadays I hardly feel like an alien at all. I'm tight with the doormen and everything. Recently it struck me that the principles I was so proud of might have been nothing grander than skirmishes in my ongoing war against Lew and Lu. Examples of superannuated adolescent rebellion."

"Your parents have the same name?"

"Lewis with an e, and Luba. Don't you love the name Luba? It's even more Jewish than Stacey."

"It's an old-world name. Goes with Vienna. And your furniture."

"You're drawn to the exotic? You see me as the alluring Other?"

"The first day at the Scoring I thought you were funny and smart. Allure had to wait until I saw you exercising."

"Exercising!"

"Mainly, though not exclusively, it was the back of your neck."

She stopped laughing, stopped meeting his eyes. "How Japanese of you."

"Japanese?"

"They're deeply into necks. Not as deeply as they're into electronic gadgets and noisemakers, of course. Crazy, isn't it? How things sort out? The whole world has to throb incessantly with canned noise or Nippon will starve."

Accept this evasion too fast, Dodge warned himself, and you'll never get her back. "Were we discussing international trade?"

She glared at him. "Don't you think it's pathetic? Millions of years of human quest and struggle leading to this? Canned noise around the clock?"

He agreed it was pathetic.

She seemed about to say more, then changed her mind.

"Could we have a walk along the river?" he asked. "I need to get the wheels off my feet."

He stood, trying to seem confident that she'd join him, and, after a moment, she did. Wordlessly they put on coats and tied scarves. The big leather shoulder bag Dodge remembered from the Scoring hung heavily from the doorknob of the coat closet. She moved to grab it, then stopped.

"If you don't want to lug that, I've got my wallet," Dodge said.

She hesitated again. Then, giving him an odd little smile, she slung the bag across her chest and opened her front door.

Chapter 30

They walked a brisk hour, talking mostly about her work at Hunter and the city that roared around them like stormy surf. Dodge confessed that New York turned him into an instant hick. But you grew up in a city, Stacia protested. No, he said, Boston's dinky, an overgrown village. This is the real thing. Real? Stacia said. This mega-artifact? This final exemplification of man-made? In summer, she said, in the streets, people getting sprinkled think it's air-conditioners. Never rain. Has to be a downpour before anyone thinks rain. Probably the only thing New York is *not*, she said, is real.

In good humor, then, faces red and sinuses clear, they approached Stacia's street door. Dodge had half-intended to say goodbye right there, but she urged him to come up, get warm, catch the last of the sunset.

Darkness had fallen, leaving the river romantically aspangle and the Jersey hills studded with light. Stacia's living room was lit by one lamp and the exuberant combustion of seasoned logs. She sat crosslegged on a hearthrug patterned intricately with deep blues and rosy salmons. Dodge's chair, upholstered in salmon, was placed so that he could enjoy the fire and the river at the same time.

They were drinking well-chilled Orvieto. "Someone

gave me this," said Stacia, disparaging the space-age plastic wine cooler.

Her attitude toward her possessions interested Dodge. From various remarks she'd made, he'd gathered that she considered not just electronic noisemakers but all material goods to be a kind of pollution. Landfill. Landfill that fetched up on her doorstep might as well stay, and like the furniture or the wine cooler, be put to use. Fundamentally, though, less would be more. Which probably explained her minimalist wardrobe.

With one of her long, dancer's stretches, she refilled his glass.

"How'm I supposed to leave if you keep doing that?"

"What's so great about Jersey?" she said, pouring some wine for herself.

"Room at the inn," he said, shrugging. "You spending Christmas with Lew and Lu?"

"I've contracted for lunch. Period. Not our holiday anyway, of course, but Luba grabs every fresh excuse to shop. Listen, I know your mother's out of the picture, but what about your father? Or brothers and sisters?"

"I'm an only child."

"Oh. Me too."

"Has its hellish aspects, doesn't it. As for my old man, I haven't seen him in years. Which seems to be okay with both of us. He's your total Californian. Esalen, the works. Daddy Hot Tub. Daddy Moonbeam."

"How many husbands did you say your mother's had?"

"Three. But she's Bud's fourth wife."

"Are WASP divorces as heedless as they sound?"

"I guess. In *The Social Register*, the women's former husbands' names are listed in parentheses after her current name. No one seems to mind trailing around a long string of exes."

"Do they list the men's former wives?"

"Men don't change their names."

"Ah. Still, though. Say you're a man, you're marrying this woman. Why would you want her past mistakes spread out for all to see?"

"Must have some connection to property. Most puzzles do."

"Here's a puzzle that doesn't. Or at least I don't think so. Why are you so ambivalent about your friends in New Jersey?"

"This." He indicated the fire and wine. "You."

She ducked her head and didn't answer.

"Uh-oh. Have I done it again? Do I feel a nip in the air?"

This brought a delighted yell of laughter. "That's Lew's favorite joke. What will people say when Japan sends up its first astronaut? There's a Nip in the air."

Her adorable bursting mouth. He slid to the floor to kiss her.

They fit. Under the wine, the taste of her mouth was sweet and clean. Her supple body came close in ways that made him feel strong and sure of himself. We will fall into bed, he thought, as Hawthorne's apples fell in honeymoon Concord—from the mere necessity of perfect ripeness. Then, gradually but unmistakeably, she seemed to change her mind.

He tried to change with her, to hold her as if in support, not to detain or force. She kept pulling away, pulling into herself. Propped on their elbows, not quite touching, they lay staring at the bright embers of the fire.

"No one's ever been here before," she finally said. "A man, I mean."

No man had touched her, she was saying, since that guy had broken in and roughed her up. Which must be what had spooked her at lunch when he'd started talking about the back of her neck.

171

The part of Dodge that had kept him a bachelor all these years reared in terror. The rest of him hung in. Touched, honored to have been chosen by her.

Did she want to be alone now, he asked. Should he leave? No, she said, no. She didn't want that at all. It was just that she couldn't promise how she'd respond if—

"You know what I think?" he said when it was clear she would say no more. "I think we should get some pillows and just lie here, enjoying the fire, talking, doing whatever we want."

"I think that too. Except you want to fuck. And I want you to want to, except—"

He kissed her lightly. "We've got plenty of time."

"We do?"

"I should have said I do."

"Unless you go to New Jersey."

"They're doing their thing with their kids. The tree and the stockings and all. They were nice enough to say I'd be missed if I didn't spend days and days with them, but they'd understand if I got a better offer."

"Dream friends."

"Yes." He leaned over and pressed his mouth to the back of her neck. Again, everything fit. Her skin felt like satin and tasted slightly salty. Her dark hair smelled like lemon.

Later, still dressed, lying on her nice big bed, its headboard witness to her grandparents'—thrilling concept!— Danubian nights, Stacia said something doomful about her small breasts. With thought, word and deed, Dodge let her know that they were rosy pippins, nectarines, cup custards, bon-bon mouthfuls of delicious delight. After that, it was clearer to her what she wanted—to snuggle under the covers with him and fall asleep, naked, warm and close.

But first she touched his erection with tender, fleeting fingers. "Are you okay?" she asked.

"Wonderfully," he said.

She frowned. "I thought men had to come."

"We agreed that we have lots of time."

Seeing that she still looked worried, he smiled at her. "Nature has her little ways. At the Scoring, I had a wet dream. The result, I'm convinced, of too much restraint in the ballroom."

"Aw."

"I'm serious. Once I'd become aware of the awesome power of your neck, it's amazing I got any work done."

"I love it that you told me. It makes me think we'll be all right together. That it's possible, I mean."

"Well sure. Aren't we all right now?"

Chapter 31

Christmas Day, Stacia crossed Central Park to have lunch with her parents.

Left alone, Dodge was aware of a strange hush. The whole building seemed deserted; no sounds rose from the street below. He might be the last man alive on earth.

You're my first man, she'd said last night, blinking back tears. My first, my *first*. The day before, when they'd not yet made love, they had decided to give each other themselves for Christmas. Like children, they had found it impossible to wait for morning. Perhaps because of this,

Dodge's unwrapping and opening of Stacia touched in him layers of long-forgotten innocence. For once, he had been able to take with a whole heart, to give as fearlessly. Santa Claus was real. Choirs of angels sang gloria.

Before they had been able to come to this exchange of gifts, they had to put themselves through the refiners's fire. It was the second day of Dodge's visit. Stacia busy with afternoon errands, Dodge had gone to Fairway, buying three kinds of mushrooms, sugar snap peas, cherry tomatoes that actually had some taste, broccoli, imported Parmesan and fresh fettucini. The pasta primavera he crafted from all this was declared superb by Stacia. So was the wine he had gambled on, an inexpensive Minervois.

Into the second bottle, Dodge found himself confessing to Stacia that he had failed Courtney and feared that he might, in time, fail others. Instead of replying, she dropped her face into her hands and blurted her own darkest secret—she hadn't just been roughed up by that man who had broken into her other apartment. She'd been raped.

"Filth," she then pronounced in her doomful way. "Brought it on myself, right? Living that way?"

"Stacia."

"You're sorry for me."

"I'm outraged. But what I feel for you, right now, is admiration and desire. I love your smells and tastes and the way you move your body. I love it that you make me laugh."

She wouldn't look at him.

He reminded her that she hadn't yet said what she thought of him. "A man who failed a kid who was counting on him. Who might fail you."

Shock yanked her out of hiding. "Not comparable."

"No," he said gently. "Courtney's dead."

"I wanted to die."

He reached for her hands and kissed them. "I hope you understand exactly how glad I am that you didn't."

"You better hear the rest. It's like Ara's explorer joke. First the legal-Kalaka—the horror that you can't even have a shower until the cops finish doing their thing. Mug-shot-Kalaka, which never led anywhere near a positive identification. Blood-test-Kalaka. When they told me I was negative for AIDS I didn't dance in the street. I got another test, waited another two weeks. Still negative. A silver lining that was balanced by abortion-Kalaka. Rape counseling, which helped, and shrinkage, which helped some more. But you know what finally brought me out? I bought a gun and learned to shoot. Some Kalaka there too, by the way. You'd be amazed how hard it is to own a gun in this city."

"Really? In the papers New York reads like a free-fire zone."

"It's not *registered* fire. Not mine, anyway. The gun goes wherever I do, but so far I haven't had to use it."

"Your shoulder bag."

"Yes."

"Wow. You had your gun at the Scoring?"

"An old friend of Lew's in Boston greased through a Massachusetts permit for me. I'm a crack shot. Once a week I go up to Rockland County to practice. I can't say I enjoy it, exactly, but I never sleep better than after I've been shooting. Don't get the wrong idea, though. My gun's a tactic, not a permanent solution. Also an eye-opener. You know what they say—a neoconservative is a liberal who's been mugged. Somewhere over the rainbow I might get back to normal. Come on, let's watch our movie. Bring the wine."

They'd rented *Swingtime*. It was Astaire's Bojangles number that made them decide to exchange themselves as gifts. Humankind is wretched and flawed. Life is a gyp, soiled by grief, humiliation and danger. But life—impossible to deny it!—is also harmony, grace. Fred and Ginger, living beings, mired like the rest of us in the human condition, lift our souls and redeem us.

Wild horses couldn't keep joy and optimism from breaking through. In the Age of Faith, this redemption would have been met by prayer and plainsong. In Postmodern Manhattan, Stacia and Dodge celebrated more directly.

It was close to four. Soon Stacia would return from her parents' lunch party. Prescott would have finished his afternoon nap.

Although the old man picked up on the first ring, he sounded less perky than usual. Christmas Eve, he told Dodge, Jason started a hunger strike. No, no, Dodge certainly should not interrupt his holiday. What would be the point? The boy seemed bound and determined to make bad worse. Teddy Massack said he was a fanatic. But what did Dodge make of the weather? Ever seen the like? It had gotten up to sixty this afternoon. In Madison! Greenhouse effect, everyone was saying. What a world we live in. They wouldn't even let you enjoy a respite from winter anymore.

Stacia's key scratched the lock. She slumped theatrically against her door, dropping two loaded shopping bags to the floor.

"All this junk—I had to take a cab. Do I smell?"

Dodge sniffed. "Only good."

"No cigarettes? No perfume?"

"Some cigarette. In your hair. Nothing to worry about, Stacia."

"Harvey and Bea—my parents' oldest friends—are chainsmokers. I've got a million Marlboros jumbled up in my nose with Lew's Aramis and Lu's Caleche. Smells really get to me. Lew thinks I should forget teaching and train as a winetaster. Claims I can make a fortune. Remember Jimmy Durante? 'The nose knows'? My nose knows it can't stand another minute. Wait'll I catch a shower."

Wrapped in one towel, drying her hair with another, she noticed Dodge's expression.

"Why so glum, chum?"

"I missed you.

She threw off her towels and came to him, her face alight. "But I was here! The whole time!"

Stacia and Dodge reached the Beasley Center late Tuesday afternoon. Mop-up would begin at eight-thirty the following morning, and, with luck, conclude well before New Year's Eve.

"I have to call on Prescott," Dodge told Stacia. "How about coming along?"

"Fine, but why?"

"The usual. I want to show you off."

Once again, Tank was visiting his grandfather. Dodge and Stacia were hospitably welcomed and drinks were poured all around. After some chitchat about the peculiarly or dangerously warm weather, Prescott started fretting about Jason.

"He's still not eating. Skin and bones, and now he's caught cold. He could go into pneumonia any minute."

"Relax, Gramper," Tank soothed. "There's penicillin."

"Teddy says he's allergic."

"Then they'll use something else."

Prescott's dismissive hand—he apparently did not share his grandson's confidence in medical science—knocked over his glass. It bounced on the rug, splashing whiskey and scattering ice cubes. "Oh, now what?" Prescott moaned, as upset as if he'd just leaked a puddle of pee.

Hearing his distress, Stacia quickly bent to scoop up the cubes. So did Tank. When the side of her head collided with Tank's Dodge almost felt the crack himself.

Prescott went into high dither, offering ice packs, aspirin, money to pay for Stacia's bent glasses.

Tank, wincing as he explored the bump on his own head, kept saying how sorry he was.

"My fault entirely," said Stacia. "And look. It's only the nose piece. I'll just bend it back. There. All set." But the smile she was giving Prescott seemed strange to Dodge. More out of kilter than her glasses.

"Fresh air," Dodge decided.

"Yes, yes. Take her home. Ice and aspirin, that's the ticket."

But Stacia, once in Dodge's rented car, wanted urgently to talk. By the time they reached the Center's parking lot, Dodge had plenty to say too.

Time forgotten, they were still hard at it when a knock on the fogged car window made them jump. Dodge rolled down the window.

"Hi lovebirds. Thought I'd mention the dinner bell."

It was Frank St. Leger, sweaty from powerwalking.

Chapter 32

In the dining hall, they spotted Di Royce, looking more beautiful than ever. And there was Mark Agresti, and Joe Callahan. "I feel exactly like an old girl," Stacia said to Dodge, "back for another season of sleepover camp."

"Sleepover?"

"What, WASPs don't have day camps?"

Tension, Dodge was learning, sharpened his lover's tongue. "Sleepover it is. Your head hurt?"

"Yes. Cramps too, since you asked."

"Ah. Well. Would booze help? Want to skip coffee and hit the lounge?"

"You go. I'll see you tomorrow morning."

He mooned at her.

"Go," she ordered, too edgy to be amused.

She was glad they'd put her on the third floor, far from the room she'd shared with Marilyn and its dangerously accessible windows. Of course, a woman who knew too much could be pushed. But she would not think of such things. If she kept her door rigorously locked, she had nothing to fear.

She had, of course, no roommate. Mop-up's chief perk.

It wasn't until ten that Tank answered the number she'd gotten from information.

"My head feels like hell," she said. "How's yours?"

He was slow on the uptake. "Oh. Hello there," he finally said.

"Can you talk? Are you alone, I mean?"

"I'm alone. What's this about?"

"Property. Inheritance. Things like that."

"I can't imagine what you're referring to."

"Dodge didn't tell your grandfather all we now know. Wanted to spare the old fellow. Marilyn Milledge was a real piece of work. Besides stealing another scholar's ideas and publishing them as her own, she's thrown around numerous accusations of sexual harassment. All lies. She's gotten people fired by telling other lies. I can document everything. And Di Royce, the woman who stomped her? I dug out the full story. That one's about as sordid as they come. The teachers who come here year after year are a nasty lot. I won't go into details. To you, I mean. But I'll be happy to tell your grandfather everything I know. Hold his nose in it until he begs for mercy."

"Yeah? Why would you do that?"

"From various things Dodge has let fall, I gather you and your grandfather disagree about the Center. I gather you have much better uses in mind for the land. Development and so forth. And why not, when it's rightfully yours?"

"Gramper doesn't see it that way."

"He doesn't want to. He prefers his fantasies—the perfectability of man through learning, bullshit like that. Dodge goes on and on, Prescott this, Prescott that, blah blah blah. But of course Dodge and your grandfather are peas in a pod. Dreamers. *Stubborn* dreamers—the worst kind. And don't forget Dodge can afford to clap and admire. He's not Prescott's own flesh and blood being sacrificed to some airy-fairy fantasy."

"My grandfather's a fool! A selfish old fool!"

"Relax. By the time I get through with him, he'll know

this place for the time bomb it is. This year, Marilyn—a trusted Table Captain, remember—sends kids notes. Next year, someone equally trusted might get on the phone. Or show up right on some kid's doorstep. A lot of them, when they write their essays, really bare their souls. Any teacher so inclined has all he needs to push their buttons, get them on his lap, do whatever he wants with them. The point is, I've got enough on this gang of frauds and perverts to turn Prescott's dreams to ashes. By the time I'm finished with them, he'll be so scared of potential lawsuits and ashamed of his delusions he'll write any will you say."

"Slight problem. I've already told him a million times the Center's full of assholes."

"Right. But you flunked out of college. Prescott's brain isn't organized to connect with people who flunked out of college. I'm different. I was Phi Beta Kappa, summa cum laude. I'm Dr. Steiner, tenure track. That means I'm *in*, Tank. Heart and soul. Prescott will know that. He'll listen to me. I can come on claiming ideals identical to his. If I say the Center is a flagrant and dangerous violation of what he and I both believe in, he's got to pay attention. All you can do is toss grenades from a position of nil credibility. I'm total credibility. And don't forget, I can document everything. Every pile of shit. From all four sexes. Make that five—bi counts too."

At Tank's end, silence.

"It's a good deal, Tank. No risk to you at all. We need a lawyer, of course. Can't do anything in this country without a lawyer. Got a yellow pages there? The lawyers're listed between pages 934 and 993. Pick a page number, come on, quick, it's got to be random selection. OK, 980. You want the first one listed or the last? OK, that's Lapham, Chester. Tomorrow morning you call Mr. Lapham, tell him to draft us an agreement. After I approve the agreement and we sign it, I pay my visit to Prescott. You'll

181

know when I've talked to him. He won't ever be the same again, I guarantee it. And the Beasley Center will be finished.''

"Hold it. What's in this agreement?"

"I'm not doing this for my health, Tank."

"How much?"

"Five hundred thousand."

"You're crazy."

"Oh? This is prime real estate. My father's big in real estate, I know how it goes. Besides, you don't have to pay until you start selling acreage. Call it a finder's fee, if you want."

More silence from Tank.

"Or," Stacia pressed on, "forget we talked and let the Center stay. Let the assholes keep their playpen forever."

"What if Chester Lapham's not that kind of a lawyer? What if he's too busy?"

"Tomorrow I'll have a fifteen-minute break at ten-thirty. I'll be in my room—312. Call me and let me know what happened. If Chester's no good, we'll play yellow pages again."

"Dodge put you up to this?"

"Are you serious? Dodge is a Boy Scout. His whole thing is worshipping Prescott. And saving Jason, of course."

"Good luck to him. The kid's guilty by a mile."

"Yeah? I'm inclined to bet with Dodge. At dinner tonight he told me—this is in strict confidence, Tank—that he's solved the crime by process of elimination. Yeah, really. No proof, but he's working on that. Dodge may be a Boy Scout, but he's also very determined. He expects to nail this man—or woman; I guess it could be a woman, he didn't say—by the end of Mop-up."

"This Milledge woman, making enemies wherever she

goes—you have to ask why no one picked her off before now."

"You thinking you'll cut in ahead of me? Use what I told you tonight to make Prescott change his will? Don't bother. Your grandfather's a smart man. On some level, he knows that Marilyn's made a mishmash of his beautiful dream. More details on her won't do the job—you need the totality. And the documentation. Without the documentation you're nowhere. Trust me, Tank. You want the land. By rights, it's yours. I want the money. I was raised to have expensive tastes. Academic salaries don't cut it, so I have to keep asking my parents for help. They make me crawl for every cent. I can't take it much longer. You have lawyer Lapham or whoever put the agreement together, we both live happily ever after."

"Wait. Tell me your name again?"

After she spelled it out for him, they hung up. She jumped to her feet and began pacing. Tell me your name again. Off the wall! Off the fucking *wall*!

With effort, she stopped herself mid-career. Breathe. She must breathe. In deep, out smooth. Deeper this time, more energy on the exhale. And deeper still, and all the way out, energy, energy, feel that sternum sink. And in—

At length she noticed that her left hand was sticky. Her damn cuticle habit—she'd been scratching and chewing away as she talked. Her thumb and two fingernails welled with blood. There were smears on her new gabardine slacks, Ralph Lauren's nifty best, Luba's Christmas shopping.

Chapter 33

Not long after Stacia went up to her room, Dodge left the dining hall to do some phoning of his own.

In his notebook, he found the numbers he'd asked Teddy Massack for without knowing when or why he might need them.

Jason's mother's line was busy. He tried the dentist. Beth, Jason's girlfriend, answered. Dodge asked his question.

"I don't think I should answer that," she said. "Jason wouldn't like me talking to you."

"You want him to die, Beth? Is that what you want? Shouldn't take long. Today a bad cold, pneumonia and who knows what else right around the corner."

Once she got started, he couldn't stop her. She told him what he'd hoped to hear. Then, her voice thinning with grievance, she detailed what the past few weeks had taught her about the unfairness of life and the torment of unanswered prayers.

"Beth? Sorry, Beth, but I have to call Mrs. Armbruster right now."

"She hates me. She blames me for everything. She—"

"I'm hanging up, Beth. Sorry."

Two tries later, Mrs. Armbruster had finished her call. She seemed to have forgotten who Dodge was. "I'm the teacher who tried to stop him."

"Of your own free will."

What did she think, it was lawsuit time? "I'm feeling much better, thanks. Don't even need to sit on a rubber pillow anymore."

"Like I said, what you did of your own free will has nothing to do with me."

He gave up trying to be friendly and asked her his question.

"I'll have to pray on that."

"I'll hold."

He timed her with his watch. It took twenty-three seconds for her to get clearance. Her answer corroborated Beth's.

His heart a commotion, he called Prescott, who said that Tank had just driven off.

"Darn," said Dodge. "I wanted you both to know that I'm onto something. I think I know who killed Marilyn. Why's still a question, but I should know by the end of Mop-up."

"That's three days, isn't it? Well. Better than never. Who did it?"

"Sorry. I can't tell you."

"Why the hell not?"

"No proof. I shouldn't even have told you what I did, but you seemed so down that I decided it was worth the risk."

"Risk? What risk?"

"I'm going to have to ask you not to take this to Chief Trevor."

"Whoa, now. Julia's got to know what you're planning. That was her deal with us."

"It won't work, Prescott. I'm going to have to wing it here. If the police are involved, the case could be lost on technicalities."

"I don't like it. I can hear my lawyer yelling about liability. Suppose you end up like that other fellow?"

"Frank St. Leger? As he'll point out to anyone listening, he lived to tell his tale. I'll be okay. If I'm right about the rest, Marilyn was supposed to have lived to tell her tale too. A bad break for her—and the killer—that she hit her head wrong."

"I still don't like it."

"How's this? If nothing definite surfaces by the end of Mop-up, I'll bring everything I know to the chief."

"Damnation. I wish you hadn't told me."

"I thought I should. You and Tank had confidence in me. You spent good money sending me around the countryside."

"So it wasn't a wild goose chase after all?"

"I hope not. But cross your fingers."

"Tank mentioned tonight that you hadn't given me a bill. Boy tends to be scrupulous about other people's accounts."

"I'll bill you, don't worry. Should I tell Tank what I just told you? About what I'm trying to pull off here?"

"I'll do that myself. Tank's had me pegged for the glue factory longer than I like to recall. Serve him right to learn I'm into creative lawbreaking. Hear how I put that? 'Into'? Not bad for eighty, eh? Some free advice for you—stay close to the young. They're noisy and silly and they don't know beans. But that's like saying oxygen is an odorless, tasteless gas. What keeps you alive keeps you alive, Q.E.D. Happy hunting. Call me the minute something happens, middle of the night, whatever."

At coffee break the following morning, Stacia was in her room as promised. However anticipated, the ringing phone made her jump.

"Chester Lapham works for Garrett & Huld," Tank said. "Big downtown firm. He does tax. He offered me

Bob Shaw, an associate in contracts. I said sure. Bob's squeezing me in before he takes lunch—I told him it was time-sensitive.''

"Good work, Tank.''

"Bobby boy sounded young. Real eager beaver. I hope he knows something.''

"A simple document, what's the problem?''

"Yeah. I'm calling you a design consultant.''

"Perfect. Finder doesn't make much sense, not when you're directly descended from the original deed holder. How about calling me when you finish? No, wait, that'll be lunchtime. I'm picnicking with Dodge today.''

"They give you picnics?''

"From noon until one the Moppers are free as little birds. If we want to build a sandwich out of the nitrates on the buffet, no one stops us.''

"Cold for picnics.''

"Fresh air's the point. Dodge knows this place out of the wind—there's a little river, and a meadow. The sun's pretty warm in the middle of the day.''

"That river's the boundary of our land.''

" 'Our' land. That's graceful of you, Tank. Even if you didn't mean it that way. But if you're going to Boston, don't you have to split?''

"Jeez, yeah, look at the time.''

"Afternoon break's at three-thirty. I'll be right at this phone.''

Chapter 34

At breakfast the following morning, the continued mild weather impelled Frank St. Leger to hold forth on the ozone layer, the greenhouse effect, the suicidal artificiality of contemporary life. "Enslavement to the machine," he announced, "has brought us to the brink of ecological disaster. Take a jogger who lives in a building with an elevator. Never once does he think, hey, if I climbed the stairs I could skip the jogging. And look at people driving cars to health clubs."

Scanning the table, Frank's eye snagged on Di Royce, who seemed abstracted and paler than usual. "Isn't it absurd, Di?"

"Mm?"

"To drive to a health club? And when you get there, what do you do? You hook yourself up to a machine. A substitute for the functional, utilitarian exertions that other machines have kept you away from all day long. Plus there's this endless squandering of fossil fuels on steam rooms and saunas."

"I've never been to a health club."

"Even so, you'll grant me the perversity of—oh my God."

Di, her napkin cupped under her mouth, was vomiting her breakfast—half a corn muffin; half a cup of tea.

"Well, well," Di murmured, placing her napkin, the

mess tucked within, carefully on her plate. Then, without hurry, she left the dining hall.

Neat as a cat, decided Stacia, who was sitting at the next table. Except that Luba's cats, when they'd been at the houseplants, showed more shame.

But Stacia's dispassionate compare-and-contrast analysis was hardly typical. Within minutes, a firestorm of rumor had swept the Center. The killer had struck again, poisoning Di Royce's tea. Who else had drunk tea this morning? Wait, who said it was only the tea? Just as easy to slip something into the coffee urns. What was to stop them? What about the orange juice? Everyone drinks orange juice—

Mop-up thrown into terror and turmoil, Cliff Rasene, with shaking hands, started to dial Julia Trevor's private number. At a tap on his door, he looked up. Seeing solemn Frank St. Leger, holding something like a salver in his hand, Rasene flashed on himself as altar boy, forty years ago. Fasting had been difficult for him; he used to pray he wouldn't faint. He yearned to faint now. Drop the phone, crash to the ground, let someone else cope. "What is it, Frank? I'm trying to call the police."

"For sure. I thought the chief would want to test this."

He set down the sacrificial salver. Di's neatly folded napkin.

Even the queasiest Moppers dragged themselves to the ballrom. Duty prodded some, others were afraid to remain alone, huddled in the beds they'd sought when rumor began churning their stomachs. Their talk was agitated by conflicting premises. Poor Di, kindly souls wailed, hasn't she suffered enough already? But there was also grumbling and blame. Di Royce draws trouble like honey draws flies. Didn't she start everything? One minute Marilyn's standing there, singing away, the next minute blam? Wouldn't you call that starting things? And what about the night she took after poor Frank? Accused him of murder, just about. Right afterward, Frank's beaten within an inch of his life. I mean! Wouldn't you call that a connection? A pattern? Doesn't it all come back to Di?

Rasene was at the podium, introducing Chief Trevor. From the look of her, the chief had been working with her horses and, given the emergency, hadn't taken time to change clothes.

"I want to reassure you all," she said, "that Dr. Hoxby is satisfied that Ms. Royce is feeling much better. He's ordered tests, but he feels her present satisfactory condition makes it highly unlikely that any foreign agent in her food or drink caused her nausea this morning. He said, in fact, that if she continues to improve you can expect her back at work later this morning.

"I know that this has been upsetting and that some of you are experiencing symptoms yourselves. Dr. Hoxby is in Mrs. Dicenzo's office. Anyone wishing to see him is urged to do so immediately."

A dozen-odd Moppers rose. Stacia and some of the others appeared abashed, hesitant. Others still looked frightened, and a few, were it not for their debility, would be roaring in outrage.

"How's Stacia?" Frank asked Dodge at the lunch buffet.

"I don't know. Her door's locked. I think she's sleeping."

"She won't be picnicking today, I guess. Poor kid. Hey. How about I tag along instead?"

"No thanks, Frank. I won't be good company."

"Who is, all the time? I'll just grab myself some of that—"

"I don't *want* company, Frank."

190

"Sure, Dodger. Take it easy. Everything's cool."

When this is over, Dodge reminded himself as he wrapped his ham and tomato sandwich in a napkin and loaded an orange and two small cartons of milk into his jacket pockets, when this is over, I may never have to lay eyes on Frank St. Leger again.

Dodge had discovered his picnic place back when he was romancing Kate. A woodland path about a half-mile long, much overgrown by scrub and brambles, led to an enormous beech tree, its trunk elephant-gray, its pale brown leftover leaves barely moving in the light wind. At this ancient tree the woods opened into a fan-shaped piece of bottomland, once meadow but now studded with small firs, in the process of returning to forest. Beyond was the little river that Stacia had mentioned to Tank. From its opposite bank a hayfield gently rose to the horizon. This land, Prescott had once told Dodge, belonged to "some new fella, can't think of his name, uses it for a write-off."

The meadow facing south, at noon you could sit with your back against the beech and bask in full sun. Immediately to the west lay a dense, encroaching fir forest. The east—the second coldest winds in New England come from the east—was protected by a long, table-like outcropping of granite some eight feet high. On the other side of this ledge was a high jungle of thorny blackberry giving onto a bog that normally would be frozen hard this time of year. Today it was black mush splintering with ice, treacherous and impassable all the way to the river.

Leaning against the beech tree, chewing away at his sandwich, Dodge could be reasonably sure that anyone having business with him would use the same path he had. If this person wished to sneak up on him, approach through the meadow was impossible. An attempt to barge straight through the firs would make too much noise for surprise;

191

least likely of all was the route through the bog and black-berries.

A sneak attack, then, would come from behind. Unless Dodge had figured wrong and attack wasn't going to come at all.

He swigged some milk. The sandwich had been a bad choice. Should've remembered his mouth would be dry. Yogurt would've been easier to swallow.

The human ear, he thought, isn't set up for rear attacks. Also, the wind was southwesterly, quartering into his face. But listening wasn't his main job right now, even if, in this thawed and sodden landscape, twigs could be made to snap under an attacker's boots. His main job, today, was to appear to be eating lunch, not a care in the world. And to trust. To trust like crazy.

Dodge felt, rather than heard, the footsteps. All at once the figure loomed above him, pointing what looked like a 12-gauge shotgun at his chest.

"Hi, Tank. What're you shooting, ducks?"

"A sitting duck, maybe. Depends on you."

"On me? Why?"

"Gramper tells me you figured out how the Milledge broad died."

Dodge registered shock and alarm.

Tank gave a short laugh. "What, you trusted him to keep his mouth shut? You're a bigger asshole than he is. Okay, I'm listening. How'd she die?"

"Can I stand up? The sun's hurting my eyes."

"Tough. How'd she die?"

"Mrs. Dicenzo did it. Knocked the poor thing right off her—"

"Don't shit me. You hear? Don't *shit* me."

"All right. You want to talk friendly, let's talk friendly. But first point that thing someplace else."

"You've got it wrong, fella. You're the one who gets

told what to do, not me. Right now I'm telling you to talk."

"And if I don't?"

"I blow you to kingdom come."

Leafing through a forensic text once, Dodge had seen a photograph showing what was left of the human face after a shotgun blast. A bowl full of clots and tatters, what might be eyeballs out where there used to be ears. "I believe you, Tank. I believe you could kill me. That's why I mailed a registered letter to Teddy Massack yesterday, describing everything I know about Marilyn's death. I retained Teddy for precisely this purpose. The letter's in a double envelope, with instructions not to open it unless I disappear or am found dead. I assume Teddy will obey those instructions, but even if he takes a peek, he can't use what he learns because he's bound by confidentiality. Your secrets are safe, I'm saying, as long as I'm alive and healthy. Want to deal?"

"What do you mean, secrets? What secrets?"

"Stacia Steiner's got a terrific sense of smell," Dodge said, as if conversationally. "When the two of you knocked heads she smelled your hair stuff. Regatta. Her father used to use Regatta too. It jogged her memory—with the shock of finding Marilyn dead, she'd forgotten smelling it in her room that night. Jason's mother says he's never used Regatta or anything like it. His girlfriend claims he's morally opposed to cosmetics in any form. Which leaves you. Where were you, under the bed?"

Even with the sun in his eyes, Dodge could see Tank's reaction to the mention of Regatta. But his rally was speedy. "That's it?" he said, overdoing the scorn. "That's what you put in your letter?"

"That and a few other things," Dodge said.

" 'A few other things,' " Tank mimicked. "What bull-shit. If you really had the goods you'd go to the police."

To Julia Trevor. Who might not be in Prescott's pocket, exactly, but who nonetheless was "family," and thus easier for Tank to stonewall. "The trouble with the police, Tank, is they have all these rules and laws slowing them down. The Constitution and so forth. Any unreasonable questioning or detention and there goes their case. You'd get, I don't know, maybe an hour of questions today, an hour tomorrow, on and on. In time they'd probably wear you down, but I'm out of time. Jason's sick and getting worse."

Tank appeared to be thinking this over.

"My letter to Teddy," Dodge continued, "also contains a full report of the deal you made with Stacia Steiner. What do you think your grandfather will say about—"

Tank snapped to. Dodge heard the pump of the shotgun. The sound of death. The last thing that bowl of clots and tatters had heard on earth.

A shot, shocking in its loudness. From Tank, a yell of astonishment. Dodge dived for the shotgun and scrambled to his feet. Stacia had said she could shoot any weapon out of anyone's hands, and she had.

Tank was staring in amazement at the fleshy part of his thumb, which was welling blood. Intent on Tank, intent on the heft of the shotgun in his hands, Dodge felt, rather than saw, Stacia ease down from the ledge.

She'd been hiding up there, waiting for Tank to take the bait offered by her phone call this morning. Ostensibly this call had been a heartening chortle between allies. New mayhem at the Center, she'd gleefully told Tank. Food poisoning. To make the most of it, she intended to spend lunch fanning every flame she could find. "Had to cancel my picnic with Dodge, of course," she'd added. "Actually, I'm rather proud of my cleverness there. I set it up so that he'd lose face with me—he's sort of sweet on me, not that I've given him much grounds—if he didn't go picnicking on his own. I don't hear applause, Tank. I don't hear thanks. Do you think Dodge should overhear me causing new trouble for his dear old Prescott? All right then. You're welcome.''

Chapter 35

"Fucking bitch,'' Tank said when Stacia, braced to shoot again, stood before him. "Look what you did to my hand!''

Dodge emptied the shotgun, pocketed the cartridges, and swung the barrel hard against the granite ledge. Chances were that Stacia's bullet had made the thing inoperable anyway, but he was taking no chances. Working firepower, in his inexpert hands, could only cause trouble.

"Calm down,'' he told Tank. "It's just surface.''

"Kidding? Look at all this blood.''

"Hand him those paper napkins,'' Stacia said to Dodge. "You're quick to cry, Tank. Considering how many people you've hurt.''

"Fucking liar. You're a fine one to talk.''

"First ground rule,'' Dodge said. "Tank will watch his language. Now. Tank has just finished threatening to kill me. Aggravated assault bordering on attempted murder.''

"A set-up,'' Tank said to Stacia. "Whole thing was a fake. You never had any intention of going to my grandfather.''

Stacia nodded. "My little pretext. I needed to mention

how much Dodge liked picnics and how close he was to solving the murder.''

"Stop saying murder! Broad falls like a ton of bricks, how's it my fault?''

"Relax,'' said Dodge. "We know you didn't mean to kill. You just wanted to generate bad publicity—enough bad publicity to push Prescott into changing his will.''

"Oh boy. Where are we, creative writing class?''

"When Stacia made the Regatta connection, I remembered something you'd said at school. You were bragging that your father was going to make millions developing this land. The ancient Beasley holdings being famous in school lore, I asked you how your father could bear to sell out. 'Easy come, easy go,' you said. Part of me, I'm sorry to say, got a real kick out of that. Kissing off a King's Grant intact from the seventeenth century—I had to admire your gall. Whole business came back to me once Stacia nailed you on the Regatta. Amazing how the mind works, isn't it? OK. You'd heard from Prescott or the grapevine that Marilyn and Di weren't divulging the reason for their fight. It must have driven you crazy. Here was this golden opportunity to sour Prescott on the C.A.T.s, and it was going to blow over, vanish without a trace. Meantime, Prescott's not getting any younger. You can't sit around forever, patiently waiting for a scandal that will make the papers all by itself. You have to act—*hold it right there.*''

"I'm only getting my handkerchief,'' Tank whined. "These napkins are useless.''

"What doomed Marilyn was her celebrity,'' Dodge said after Tank finished wrapping his hand. "You figured a second, more serious attack on her would force the Center to call in the police. That, naturally, would bring in the reporters. Lots of reporters. Nationally famous person, mysterious assailant—it's a great story. Terrific color, and every possibility that Marilyn's fight with Di Royce would turn up fresh dirt.''

"Creative writing class," Tank said again.

"The rest was a gamble. Prescott might find the strength to ignore the ruckus and hang in with the Center. The main thing was that it *could* work. With the stakes so high, and the risks so low, you had to give it a shot or hate yourself forever.

"You never dreamed, of course, that she'd end up dead. Ironical, isn't it? Jason's involvement, the postcards and all, would have played into your hands perfectly—if only your first priority didn't have to be covering your ass. As soon as you dared, you were going to use Marilyn's postcards and the rest of the Center's troubles to reopen your campaign for the will change. But suppose some new evidence turned up that exonerated Jason? Now the question would be who *did* kill Marilyn? Put another way, who had the most to gain from Marilyn's death?''

"How much more of this do you expect me to listen to?''

"You had to build a wall in everyone's minds between yourself as beneficiary and the inconvenient fact of Marilyn's death. What better way than to go on record as a major supporter of Prescott's efforts to clear Jason? Which must be why you arranged the car rental for me. I thought at the time that was fishy. Why were you going out of your way, being so nice to me all of a sudden? I should have listened to my gut. All right. You got into Marilyn's room. You must have disguised yourself. How?''

"Why're you asking? You've got all the answers.''

"Clearly we need a second ground rule," said Dodge. "Tank tells the truth or we lose interest in helping him conceal his plot against his grandfather. Not to mention today's murder attempt.''

"I bought some cheap sunglasses and a windbreaker in

Zayre's. Wet my hair and combed it back with that fucking gel.''

"Gel," said Stacia. "Regatta gel. Overwhelming when wet." Which was why, mid-sneeze, she'd told her father he had to find a new brand.

But Dodge was skeptical. "That's a disguise?"

"Definitely," said Stacia, thinking of the striking transformation in Dodge's appearance the first time the two of them had sported in her New York bathtub. "Change the hairline, you change the man. Marilyn would have described someone who didn't exist. Ditto any other Reader who happened to spot him. And this someone can disappear in seconds. All he needs is a comb and a place to toss the shades and windbreaker."

Tank appeared gratified by this. Pleased with himself. Dodge couldn't believe it. Dense the guy undeniably was, but basking in the cleverness of his disguise? "One thing I've been wondering about, Tank. Why didn't Marilyn scream for help?"

"Yeah. That was weird. She came into the room limping, heavy on her feet, so I knew it was her. She turned on the TV and went into the bathroom." A boy's smirk crossed Tank's face. "Cut a couple of fierce ones in there. Pretty gross. I turned up the volume, in case she yelled, but when she came out and saw me she was like, well now, this could be fun. Nearly freaked me out."

Stacia shivered, remembering how Marilyn had sung. *Are you my life to be* . . . Gender studies, apparently, did not immunize against romantic yearnings, fantasies of conquest by a handsome stranger.

"Which leaves the real baffler," Dodge now said. "Why beat up Frank St. Leger?"

"Oh no you don't. That wasn't me."

This denial didn't surprise. Having graduated from mischief to manslaughter, Tank would hardly act so decisively to get the heat off Jason.

"Okay, forget Frank," Dodge said. "Here's the program. We walk to the Center, you, Stacia, Stacia's gun, and me. We go straight to Mrs. Dicenzo's office. No one sees the gun, but you never forget it's there, aimed to do real damage. We get Chief Trevor on the phone and you tell her you've been overcome by guilt and want to confess. Once Jason's free, Stacia and I forget the rest."

"I'm supposed to trust liars?"

"Your guarantee," Stacia said, "is Prescott. Neither of us wants him hurt more than he's already going to be."

"Gramper's never going to find out I was going to sic you on him?"

"Not from us. Tell that lawyer to tear up our contract. He works for you, no problem there."

Tank was frowning hard, weighing his options.

"You don't have much choice," Dodge said.

"All right. Let's get it over with. My hand's killing me."

Dodge doubted that Tank hoped to spare Prescott. More likely he hoped to spare himself the full measure of his grandfather's disgust and grief. Either way, he, Dodge, would take it. Tank was stupid. Brighter, he might have told his captors to stuff their offer, delivering them to the wrath of Julia Trevor. And the wrath of Prescott. Who, had he been consulted, would almost certainly have demanded they bring their case straight to the police instead of risking their own lives and adding assault or attempted murder to his grandson's burdens.

"First let's put some meat on your story," Dodge said. "You're out looking for ducks. You find us and we get talking about poor Jason on the verge of pneumonia. Stacia smells your hair stuff and says wow, Regatta. She suddenly remembers there was Regatta in the room that night and thinks she better tell Chief Trevor right away. By the way, I can't smell a damn thing. Can you, Stacia?"

Stacia came close enough, sneezed, and backed away to safety.

"Easy, Tank," Dodge soothed. "The only thing you have to think about now is how you were completely overcome by remorse. You broke down and confessed to us. You asked us to disarm the shotgun so you wouldn't be tempted to further wickedness. How's that sound, Stacia?"

"Good. Solid."

"Let's recap, then, just to clarify. Stacia and I don't like you much, Tank. You put a seventeen-year-old kid through hell. If you try any fancy moves, we'll do the same to you. When you're concocting your defense, make sure your lawyer is absolutely clear on our position. You don't want us provoked."

Again Dodge and Stacia exchanged looks. She nodded and resumed shooting stance as he started climbing the granite ledge.

From above came clicking noises, then the recorded sound of Stacia sneezing and Dodge telling Tank to take it easy. Another click and Dodge slid down, tape recorder in hand. Taping the hoped-for confrontation had been Stacia's idea.

"Insurance," Dodge informed Tank, whose face looked terrible. "The order of march is Tank first, Stacia right behind. I'll be sweep and carry the shotgun. Your bag, too, Stacia? Just until you have to hide the gun? Fine. Let's move. Slow and steady."

Following close behind Stacia, brave, wonderful Stacia, Dodge knew it was too early for relief. But he could begin marvelling at what the two of them had achieved.

They had argued, of course, the merits of playing it safe, taking their evidence to the police. What finally had settled them was that no one, Prescott included, had as sore a need as Dodge to save Jason.

And you could also marvel at the webbed complexities that had enabled their decision. Because of a man, Stacia owned a gun and knew how to use it. Because she'd dared once again to trust a man in bed, in her body, she could demand, and receive, that man's full trust at the beech tree.

Dodge's risk was much the larger, which Dodge insisted was only right. He had the most to gain. He'd just finished explaining why when Frank St. Leger came up to tap on their breath-fogged car window. "You save Jason, you expiate Courtney," Stacia had realized by the time Frank moved on. After that, she could stand in Dodge's way no longer.

Chapter 36

"As we begin this final morning," Cliff Rasene said, "I am moved to recall Dr. Johnson's assertion that people rarely say *this is the last* without some measure of uneasiness. For me, the approaching end of this much-troubled Scoring must stand as one of those rare instances.

"As many of you already know, Dr. Beasley's grandson has confessed to causing Marilyn the fall that ended her life. His aim, he has said, was to create an impression of chaos and thus persuade his grandfather to rescind the trust which allows the Center to enjoy this beautiful country setting. He insists that he did not intend to kill, but that, of course, is for the jury to decide. While I, and anyone who knows him, will feel sad for Dr. Beasley, we must also remember that Jason Armbruster has now been freed from his gravest charge. I'm sure I speak for us all when I say that I hope the rest of Jason's problems are speedily resolved as well. Several Readers have suggested to me that a scholarship fund be established for him, by way of reparation for the injuries set in motion by Marilyn's most unfortunate breach of confidentiality. The board is one hundred percent behind this idea, and you will all be contacted soon as to how you may contribute, should you choose to do so.

"On a far happier note, one of Dr. Hoxby's tests has established that Di Royce's indisposition was most likely a touch of morning sickness. Congratulations, Di, and best of luck."

A buzz of comment ran through the ballroom. Other Readers, Dodge decided, must be as astonished as he that priggish Rasene had so calmly congratulated an unmarried woman on her pregnancy. He himself had known since breakfast, when Di, sipping weak, unsweetened tea, had told him, adding that the baby would have her and her friend Becca for parents, not Ara. "Will Ara," Dodge asked, "object to that?" "Of course not," said Di, "Ara's got plenty of daughters of his own." "You know already that the baby's a girl?" "The odds are excellent. Ara seems to make girls. You seem angry, Dodge. Why?" "I'm not angry," said Dodge, who was. Di had caused too much trouble to have landed so blithely sure of herself. "Suppose it's a boy," he went on. "Ara's first son. Mightn't he want to know him?" Di laughed. "Becca and I will deal with that if and when. You shouldn't try to pin things down so hard, Dodge. It's a waste of energy."

"There remain two mysteries," Rasene was saying.

"One is the nausea that some of you experienced yester-day. Dr. Hoxby feels that suggestion may have been the culprit—which is perfectly understandable, given the stressful conditions of this Scoring.

"The second mystery involves Frank St. Leger's at-tacker. Chief Trevor is working on this right now, with Frank himself."

Another buzz of comment. Rasene held up his hand. "We must now look to the future. It has been suggested that codes be used to identify individual essays, instead of names and addresses. This seems, to me at least, a good idea. We'll be pursuing it. Dr. Beasley's great shock has left him undecided in his plans for the center. It's possible that next year's Scoring will have to be held in a different location. I can only assure you that the C.A.T. Scoring will continue, and add that I am proud to be associated with Readers who have performed so willingly and con-scientiously under what we may call, without exaggera-tion, fire. Let's start reading."

Dodge tried his best, but his mind wouldn't latch onto Kidspeak and chained humanity. He was worried about Prescott, who had sent, through Chief Trevor, a message that Dodge should leave a phone number; he would call when he was able. Then the chief, separately and skepti-cally, had questioned Dodge and Stacia. "I *know* Tank Beasley," the chief, exasperated, had told Dodge at one point. "Breaking down like that, giving in to guilty feel-ings, all right, *finer* feelings—that's simply not Tank's thing. He's not built that way." "What can I say?" Dodge asked, not for the first time. Now, however, he suspected something new: Julia Trevor had been in love with Tank, and he had not loved her back. Would this, had Dodge and Stacia gone to her instead of taking the Regatta clue for an end-run, have made her a fierce or reluctant pros-ecutor? They'd never know.

In love himself, Dodge felt bad for any lover who had been disappointed, especially a lover who had made an unworthy choice.

Worthiness. Dodge Hackett loves, and hopes to be worthy of, Stacia Steiner.

They had plans. Since he didn't have to be back in Winnetka until September, he would stay with her in New York until summer—assuming that this continued to seem a good idea to both of them. Then they'd spend the summer traveling together. Then. . . . Then they'd see. Meantime, he'd better get to work.

There is an implicit paradox, Dodge read, *in the idea that freeborn humanity tolerates and may even consent to a life in chains. This is the paradox that Robert Frost describes in his short poem "Bond and Free." Love, says Frost, is of the earth. Love's "circling arms" "shut fear out." But we are also creatures of Thought, which "has a pair of dauntless wings." The poet leaves it to his readers to decide whether Love, by "simply staying" is more powerful than Thought, which goes anywhere, including outer space.*

A further ramification of the paradox can be seen in a small child. One minute he is crying for his mother. The next minute he is off on his own, testing his "dauntless wings."

Holy shit, thought Dodge, a live one. He read through to the concluding sentences: *Paradoxes of this nature, intrinsic to human existence, can never be resolved. The fortunate few may learn to appreciate and enjoy them; many others can only hope for the strength to endure.* Then checked the name and address. Charlotte Bardle, Bozeman, Montana.

You were supposed to bring exceptional papers to the Master Readers. Sometimes, at the end of the day, Rasene would read one aloud—the idea being that quality, however rare, redeemed the thin gruel of the norm. This theory Dodge had always considered fraudulent. Still, he was eternally grateful, right now, for Charlotte Bardle. He'd coax Rasene into bending the rules and making a copy. A gift for Prescott, something Dodge could have in hand once his old friend could bear to see him again.

Bozeman, Montana. Holy shit.

Chapter 37

Two days later, Dodge, marking time at his mother's, received the call he'd been waiting for. Prescott would see him that afternoon. "And Dodge?" the old man added. "This time don't forget your bill."

Dodge, who'd arrived in Chestnut Hill resolving to be more communicative, to act more like his real self, tried to explain to his mother and Bud why this was remarkable. "Prescott's eighty. He's had a shock that would flatten anyone. If he shot the messenger who brought the bad news, no one, including the messenger, me, that is, could blame him. Instead, he sticks these ironical little quotation marks around 'forget.' "

Diana and Bud showed a pleasant blankness. Dodge tried again. "Business is business, he was saying. Let's not clutter things up with noble gestures."

"Breeding tells," said Bud, chin stalwart, mouth pursed. Bud liked a world clearly divided into them and us.

205

"But didn't that same breeding," Dodge's real self felt obliged to wonder, "also produce Tank?"

A silence built.

"Really, darling," Diana then chided her son. "You can't blame parents for everything. It's not *fair*."

They were saved by another phone call, this one from Teddy Massack. "Prince Jason wishes me to inform you that your ceaseless importuning has touched his heart. He will grant a brief audience this afternoon."

"You still don't like him, huh."

Massack laughed. "Let's hold off on that. Until after you've had your audience."

A blue norther had swept in, the warm spell a distant memory. Inside the DYS house, though, it was hot, stuffy, strongly redolent of male animal—a compound of sweat, crotch, dirty socks and dander underlaid by something sweetish. Secreted food, maybe. Or bad teeth.

Jason, who had started eating again right after he'd heard the news of Tank's confession, still looked thin and pale. In one hand he carried his Bible, in the other a box of tissues. He must still have his cold.

He sat down and gave Dodge an encouraging smile.

Dodge also dispensed with greetings. "Mr. Massack tells me that the woman whose car you took isn't pressing charges, so there's a good chance you'll be paroled home after your hearing Monday. I think it's terrific he was able to get it scheduled so soon."

"But isn't that the least they can do? After incarcerating me for something I never did?"

"I hadn't thought of it quite that way."

"I know what you think, Mr. Hackett. You think I should be grateful. I am grateful, to my Lord and Savior Jesus Christ. Who sent you to my cause and helped you prevail against the forces of darkness and deceit. I'm glad you came to visit me today, because I want you to know that for as long a life as the Lord grants me, you will always be in my prayers. You and the other teacher.''

''Ms. Steiner. I'll tell her. Thank you, Jason.''

Jason sneezed, used one of his tissues. ''My deepest prayer will be for your souls to be lifted and comforted by the Holy Spirit.''

''Thank you again. What lies ahead for you, Jason? I hope you're still excited about going to college.''

''Oh definitely. You know, people who aren't Christians go around thinking we're sort of retarded. But the fact is that when the Lord blesses us with gifts, He means for us to use them. Of course we can't know exactly what His intentions are. We must pray for His help and guidance.''

''You'll still pursue math, though, won't you?''

''As long as the Lord wants me to, yes.''

''I'm curious. What's your first choice college?''

''I don't have a first choice. Harvard, Yale, MIT, they're all pretty good.''

Dodge conquered an impulse to ask if Princeton was his safety school. ''Could we clear up one last thing? What exactly did Ms. Milledge's postcard say?''

''I won't utter blasphemy.''

''I understand.'' Dodge tore paper from his notebook and passed it to the boy with his pen. ''But how about writing it out for me?''

''Blasphemy is poison! No matter how it enters your system! I don't want to poison you, Mr. Hackett.''

''I appreciate that. On the other cards she sent, she used quotations. I gathered from your reaction to my grand-mother's—right, we don't have to go into that again. That was Ben Franklin, I've since learned. Did Ms. Milledge quote anyone else to you?''

''Please, Mr. Hackett. I don't want to think about it.''

''Just this once and never again. I really need to know.''

With great reluctance, Jason bent over the notepaper and, bearing down hard, wrote a few lines.

Men never do evil so completely and cheerfully, Dodge read, *as when they do it from religious conviction (Pascal).*

Jason misunderstood his frown. "I tried to tell you, Mr. Hackett. I tried to warn you how terrible it was. No wonder the Lord sent me to her."

"Sent you? Do you mean that literally?"

"Of course. I'd never have the nerve to do what I did on my own."

"Back up a little. You read the card and thought, uh-oh, lousy grade."

"Anyone who would mock the Lord so totally would have to despise a believer."

"Do you know who Pascal was?"

"I know there's a computer language called Pascal. But they couldn't be the same person."

"Why not?"

"Because this is a terrible blasphemy!"

"They're the same person. Pascal was a brilliant mathematician and scientist. Seventeenth century. He also wrote an important work of religious philosophy. You'd do well to take a look at it."

Jason smiled and lifted his Bible. "Here's *my* religious philosophy, Mr. Hackett. Here's the only truth humans ever need."

"It may not be that simple."

"But it *is* simple. When Jesus is your Lord and Savior, everything is simple."

Dodge couldn't stand it. "Suppose Harvard and the rest turn you down. What then? The Lord tells you to go after the Deans of Admissions? Kidnap their children?"

"You just don't get it, do you, Mr. Hackett."

"What I get is that the Lord told you to do what you wanted to do anyway, including steal a car."

"Like I said, Mr. Hackett, I'll pray for you."

Kid's only seventeen, Dodge reminded himself. Lay off. Don't play Bishop of Beauvais to his Joan of Arc. Kind of life he's had, simplistic claptrap's probably all he can handle.

Besides, the audience was over. Bible pressed to heart, eyes closed, lips busy, Jason had checked out.

A parting shot? "Read Pascal," Dodge tried. "Keep safe. Grow up."

Jason gave no sign of hearing.

Back in his rental, heading for Prescott's, Dodge thought some more about Joan of Arc, who'd been burned for insisting that heavenly voices guided her every move. Thanks to Jason, the next time Dodge assigned his seniors Shaw's *St. Joan*, he'd bring new insight to the class discussion. Of *course* the Bishop wants to wring Joan's neck, he'd tell the kids. What's remarkable is that the Bishop doesn't— that somehow he finds the will to restrain himself, to wait for a more ceremonious release.

Chapter 38

Prescott had a fire going, the drink tray arranged as usual. "Doris thought you might want tea. It's all set up in the kitchen. Just turn the kettle on."

"Bourbon's fine. Shall I?"

"Please. And give me just a splash of that siphon. Nice to have siphons back, isn't it?"

209

"Very nice."

"I saw a glass one in a catalog. Wire mesh, everything. Might spring for one if nostalgia gets the better of me. They send me three, four, catalogs a day. Must cost them a fortune. Foolish. Man my age either has a full quota of impediments or has learned to do without. I'm babbling. You're not here to talk about catalogs."

"No."

"When I sent you out on the road I hoped you'd turn up a jealous boyfriend. An outsider. I didn't want it to be one of the Readers or Center staff. Or poor Jason, of course. Well. Here we are. You brought your bill?"

Dodge presented it. Prescott went to his desk. He used a fountain pen and a rocking blotter. From the back, he seemed older, frail enough to put a lump in Dodge's throat. The writing on the check was shaky but fully legible.

"Julia's implied in various ways that the District Attorney will settle for manslaughter, eight years minimum. Tank might manage good behavior and be out in five. I'll be dead or eighty-five. He'll be thirty-eight. I was twenty-five when his father was born."

"People marry later now."

"Beasley's not the easiest handle to carry around. Know what they called me in school? Knees. For bee's knees. We had that kind of expression then. Bee's knees. Cat's pajamas. It meant you were all right. Pretty good, in fact. My son was called Measly. Tank was Weasel. Pattern of deterioration, wouldn't you say? I used to wish I'd produced more children. That my son had too. Improve the odds of getting a couple of good ones. Now I don't know. I just don't know."

"Tank could straighten up."

Prescott gave him a hard look: no bullshit. But Dodge could not leave his old friend comfortless, so he groped ahead. "For me, the worst is losing hope. That flat, dead sense—even false or impossible hopes are better than that. I'm making a mess of this. What I think I mean is, you've always been an optimist, Prescott. An idealist. Teachers can be pretty cynical. You should hear us laughing over the kids' dumb mistakes. Partly it's to keep from crying over their goddamn *inertness*. Their horrible acquiescence to the worst of the status quo—the getting and spending they call the good life. It's hard, as a teacher, to find chinks, to find new ways to wake kids up to the idea that life can be more than going to the shopping mall. We try, though. We persist in thinking we can make a difference.''

Dodge stopped, but Prescott apparently was not yet ready to respond. ''Course, some of us,'' he went on, ''can match the most inert kid that ever lived. We're worse because we're older. Hardened. Some teachers, you have to hope the kids use the hour to read comics or sleep.''

''Lies and illusions.''

''Sorry?''

''Dostoevsky said man is a creature who walks on two legs and is ungrateful. And deceives himself, I'd add. I'm not talking about big lies—environmental lies, or the stuff the Pentagon puts out and we deceive ourselves into believing. I'm too old to mount much of a challenge on that level. But I think that I'd been living without too much personal lying. Until this business with Tank.''

''Is believing in education what you mean by a personal lie?''

''No, no. At worst, a hopeful illusion. As you say, we need to feel we're making a difference. But I've had to face something. I created the Center out of disappointment with my son. No man with a son like mine can remain persuaded that his bloodline is worth beans. Or that inheritance—whether of goods, land or genes—offers much hope of progress. So I turned egalitarian. I created the

C.A.T.s for youngsters who value what my own family spits on.''

"Damn good thing you did, too. Ask any bright kid who happens to have been born in a slum. Or some dinky little burg miles from a decent library.''

"You really believe that?''

I really believe, Dodge said to himself, that I want to leave you comforted. "I couldn't go on teaching if I didn't. I brought you this, from Bozeman, Montana.''

He handed over Charlotte Bardle's essay.

Prescott read through to the end. Then, smiling for the first time that afternoon, he thanked Dodge.

"Says it all, doesn't it?'' Dodge asked.

"Certainly it says why I've been proud of the C.A.T.s and the Center. But I'd be prouder of myself if my original motive had been something better than the ashes of family disappointment.''

Dodge nodded his understanding.

Prescott asked Dodge to top off their drinks. While Dodge did this, he mentioned to Prescott that they hadn't yet talked about Frank St. Leger.

"Lordanharry, so we haven't. You know, I'm still not sure Cliff Rasene should have announced it.''

"Oh, I think he was right to. People were grumbling about his concealment of the postcards. Scared, too. Ready to magnify whatever loose ends were left—which might have made trouble in years ahead.''

Tank's denial had forced Julia Trevor to question Frank more closely than she had before. First she made him go through his story again. Then he had to retrace his steps at the scene, not once but twice. Then, in her office, she asked him to write the whole thing out, step by step. This apparently, had done the trick. Starting to cry, he'd told the truth.

His beating had been self-inflicted, the first blow struck

by the trunk of a tall oak he couldn't see in the dark. Surprise and pain had instantly delivered to him the means by which he might redeem what Di Royce had stripped away. He swung his mouth hard into the oak until he tasted blood. Then he raked his fingernails down his cheek. Stacia later would tell Dodge she had no trouble imagining every minute. "It's what victims have for joy," she'd said, shuddering. "The ecstasy of self-abasement."

"Tank has been carefully mute on the entire subject," Prescott now said. "No told-you-so's, even though yet another of my beloved teachers has proved less than honorable. Earlier you said Tank might mend his ways. Perhaps he's started. Might as well try to believe that, eh? How's your drink?"

"I'm fine. I have to be getting back soon."

"I'm glad your mother lives near Boston. When you're visiting her, come see me."

Not wanting to burden Prescott with the idea that one visit a year, piggybacked onto the Scoring, was enough for both Diana and her son, Dodge said he was going to be in New York for awhile, with trips to New England a real possibility.

The two men stood and shook hands.

"Until next time, then," said Dodge.

"Until next time. I've been thinking I should sell some land. Couple of house lots on the southern border. This idea I've been dragging around that I have to preserve the whole grant absolutely intact is starting to look like pure stubbornness. No one's going to miss a couple of lots, and the money will let me beef up the endowment. Fix the pool and so forth."

"Be nice to have the pool back. Like siphons."

"Yes. Maybe you'll do something for me, next year. Jot down some of those funny things the kids come up with. No harm in a laugh or two."

"I'll type out this year's best and send them to you."

"You remember them?"

"Sure. They're indelible. I'll give you a taste. A young man named Chou drew a reference from Shakespeare. King Real, he wrote, was chained by his quick temple."

"King— Oh Lord. Oh that's wonderful."

"That's just a sample. I'll get some more to you soon as I can."

They laughed again, said goodbye, and Dodge was off.

White-haired grandmother...

&

free-lance CIA agent...

DOROTHY GILMAN'S
Mrs. Pollifax Novels